Everything you ever wanted to know
—and more—
about

WORLD'S MOST ELIGIBLE BACHELOR
Cal Langtry

Occupation:	"Filthy-rich oil tycoon. And brand-new father of a twelve-year-old girl—it's a long story...."
Plans to Settle Down:	"Guess I'll have to turn in my bachelor ways and make a home for my daughter. But it sure won't be easy becoming a family man."
Potential Bride:	"Most women I know are interested in my money, not motherhood. Though there is my able assistant, Sabrina, who could give me some parenthood pointers."
Marriage Vow:	"Now my assistant's got me wanting to mix business with pleasure. Guess we'll have to see...."

Dear Reader,

Thank you for joining us for another WORLD'S MOST ELIGIBLE BACHELORS book. This brand-new series brings you twelve of the sexiest heroes in the world—written by some of the most stellar authors in the romance genre.

Every month, fictitious *Prominence Magazine* names one of their World's Most Eligible Bachelors. We'll follow the story of that desirable male and discover all the intimate details of how he finally trades in his bachelor status for a wedding ring.

This month, bestselling author Susan Mallery turns up the heat with her *Lone Star Millionaire,* Cal Langtry. He may come from "old" Texas money, but he's got a brand-new job as daddy to a daughter he never knew existed. Now all this confirmed bachelor needs is a woman willing to teach him the true meaning of family.

And be sure to catch next month's bachelor, Kieran O'Hara. This *Agent of the Black Watch* was created by beloved author BJ James, and is part of her bestselling THE BLACK WATCH miniseries in Silhouette Desire. Be careful, readers, or this secret agent lover just might steal your heart.

Until next time…here's to romance wishes and bachelor kisses!

The Editors

Please address questions and book requests to:
Silhouette Reader Service
U.S.: 3010 Walden Ave., P.O. Box 1325, Buffalo, NY 14269
Canadian: P.O. Box 609, Fort Erie, Ont. L2A 5X3

World's Most
Eligible Bachelors

Susan
Mallery
Lone Star
Millionaire

Silhouette Books

Published by Silhouette Books
America's Publisher of Contemporary Romance

SILHOUETTE BOOKS

ISBN 0-373-65027-2

LONE STAR MILLIONAIRE

Copyright © 1998 by Susan W. Macias

This edition published by arrangement with Harlequin Books S.A.

® and TM are trademarks of Harlequin Books S.A., used under license.
Trademarks indicated with ® are registered in the United States Patent
and Trademark Office, the Canadian Trade Marks Office and in other
countries.

Printed in U.S.A.

A Conversation with...
Bestselling author
SUSAN MALLERY

What hero have you created for WORLD'S MOST ELIGIBLE BACHELORS, and how has he earned the coveted title?

SM: Cal Langtry is a Texas oilman—handsome, charming and a wizard when it comes to making money. He's also a sworn bachelor...and practically every single lady still breathing would love to find his cowboy boots next to her bed.

What kind of heroine did you create to snag your WORLD'S MOST ELIGIBLE BACHELOR?

SM: Sabrina is Cal's assistant. Over the years she's become his best friend and occasionally his conscience. He's about to find out that the thought of losing her is going to change how he looks at the world in a huge way.

What about WORLD'S MOST ELIGIBLE BACHELORS appealed to you? Do you have any other special titles readers can look for?

SM: I love the idea of a series about bachelors. Men who have sworn to remain single often make the best kind of heroes. In real life, women want men who are warm, sensitive and looking for a commitment, but in romance fiction we seem to prefer hard-driven males who have to be tamed before they can fall in love.

BRIDES OF BRADLEY HOUSE, a new Silhouette Special Edition duo, launches in March 1999 with *Dream Bride*. The second book, *Dream Groom*, is a May 1999 release. Other Special Edition titles will follow in 1999.

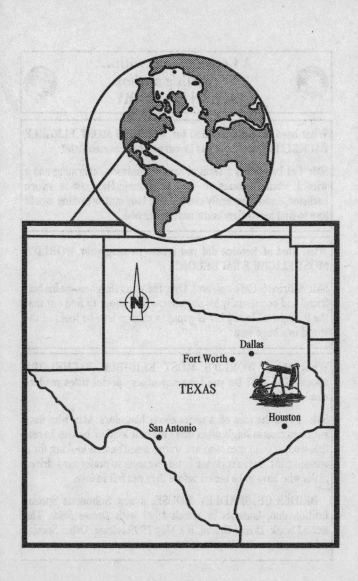

Dallas

Fort Worth

TEXAS

Houston

San Antonio

One

"Madam must agree that it's very beautiful," the store clerk said.

Sabrina Innis stared down at the diamond tennis bracelet glinting on her wrist. "Madam agrees," she told the well-dressed young man, then glanced at her boss. "Stunning. And ten carats, too. Are you sure you wouldn't rather buy her a little car? It would be cheaper."

Calhoun Jefferson Langtry, all six feet three inches of him, raised his eyebrows. "I'm not interested in cheap. You should know that by now. I want to send something meaningful, but elegant." He motioned to the diamond pin the clerk had first shown them. "Nothing froufrou, though. I hate froufrou."

The "froufrou" in question was an amazing diamond-and-gold pin that cost what the average family of four earned in three or four months. It had clean lines, a zigzag ribbon of gold dividing a stylized circle, with a large four-carat diamond slightly off center. Sabrina loved it and would have chosen it in a hot minute. But the gift wasn't for her.

She unclasped the tennis bracelet and placed it next to the other finalists—a gold bangle inlaid with diamonds and emeralds, and a Rolex watch. "I sense a theme here," she said. "Things that go around the wrist. Shackles, in a manner of speaking. Is this your way of telling Tiffany that she shouldn't have tried to tie you down?''

Her impertinence earned her a scowl. She smiled back. Cal's temper existed mostly in his mind. Compared to the screaming in her house when she was growing up—four siblings all with extreme opinions on everything—his mild bouts of ill humor were easy to tolerate. Not that the man couldn't be stone cold when it suited him. She made sure never to cross him in important issues and counted these tiny victories as perks of the job. If nothing else, they kept her wit sharp—a definite advantage when dealing with the wealthy and privileged.

"This one," she said, pointing to the emerald-and-diamond bracelet.

The clerk paused, waiting for Cal's approval.

"You heard the little lady. Wrap it up."

"Yes, sir."

Sabrina rose to her feet. After six years of being in Texas, she'd grown used to being called "little lady." She often accused Cal of being trapped in a John Wayne western. Not that he couldn't be urbane when he chose. When it suited his purposes, he could talk about world events, pick out the perfect wine and discuss the changing financial market with the best of them. But with her, he was himself—Cal Langtry, rich, Texas oil tycoon and playboy. She looked at the piece of jewelry the clerk tucked into a velvet box. A soon-to-be unattached playboy.

"Does Tiffany know?" Sabrina asked as Cal signed the credit card receipt. The clerk held out the bag, not sure to whom to hand it. Sabrina took it. Even though the gift wasn't for her, she was responsible for mailing it to the recipient, after she'd composed a suitable note.

Cal led the way to the front of the store, then held open the door for her. "Not exactly."

Sunlight and the spring heat hit her full in the face. Despite having lived here six years, she still wasn't used to the humidity. She felt her hair start to crinkle. So much for the smooth, sophisticated style she'd tamed it into that morning. The hair-care industry had yet to invent a hair spray that could outlast the Houston weather.

They crossed the sidewalk to the waiting limo. As always, Cal politely waited until Sabrina had settled into the seat. She liked to think it was because he enjoyed watching her skirt climb up her thighs. The truth was, he never bothered to look.

It was better that way, she told herself, wondering when she was going to start believing it. After all, if she was as good-looking as her boss, they would cause a stir wherever they went and all the attention would grow annoying. As it was, she was able to slip into the background and live her life in peace and quiet.

She chuckled softly and glanced out the window.

"What's so funny?" Cal asked.

"I was wondering if we were going to have a storm this afternoon," she said. It was almost the truth. She'd really been wondering if her outrageous lies, told only to herself, would cause her to be struck by lightning.

She set the carefully wrapped gift between them. "Tiffany's for Tiffany," she said, pointing to the name on the bag. "I wonder if your soon-to-be ex-girlfriend will appreciate the irony."

"Don't start with that, Sabrina," Cal warned. "Tiffany was a splendid girl."

"I couldn't agree more."

He eyed her, as if he didn't believe what she was

saying. "Okay, so she wasn't the brightest person on the planet," he admitted.

"Now, there's an understatement."

He narrowed his gaze.

Sabrina feigned fear by sinking back into the corner of the limo. "Oh, Mr. Langtry, please don't punish me for my impertinence. I'm just the hired help. I desperately need this job to support my orphaned brothers and sisters. I'll do anything to get into your good graces."

She fluttered her eyelashes for effect.

Cal faced front. "Dammit, Sabrina, I hate that I can't stay angry with you. Why is that?"

"Why do you hate it or why can't you stay angry?"

"Both."

"You can't stay angry because I'm nearly always right, and you can't hate it because deep in your heart you know I'm incredibly bright. Smarter than you, even. So you spend your days intimidated by me but determined not to let me know."

"In your dreams." He pointed at the bag. "Why'd you pick that bracelet over the other one or the watch?"

She stared at him. "Do you want the truth?"

"Oh, so I'm not going to like your reasoning. Sure. Tell me the truth."

She shrugged. "Tiffany is a sweet girl, but young. Her taste is a little, shall we say, undeveloped. While the diamond bracelet was beautiful, I thought it would be too plain. The emeralds give the bangle flash and she'll like that."

"Agreed. Why not the watch?"

"We're talking about Tiffany here, Cal. The watch

wasn't digital, and I'm not completely convinced she can tell time the old-fashioned way."

"Remind me to fire you when we get back to the office."

"You asked me for the truth."

"So you're telling me it's my fault?"

"You're the one who chose Tiffany, and now you're the one who doesn't want to deal with the hassle of ending it. What do you want the card to say?"

He shifted on the seat. "Something nice. That we had a great time together, but we don't want the same things. You know. The usual. And stop looking at me that way."

"What way?"

"Like you disapprove. Your face gets all scrunchy. It's not attractive."

Sabrina resisted the urge to whip out her compact and peer at herself. She doubted that she was the least bit scrunchy, but she hated not knowing.

"I don't have an opinion on your personal life."

"Liar," he countered. "Why are you always telling me what to do and always disapproving of the women I pick?"

"Tiffany was all of twenty. You're using the term *woman* very loosely. I'd be willing to accept *mature girl*, or even *postadolescent*. If you actually picked a woman, I might not disapprove."

"Colette was nearly twenty-eight. That counts."

He had a point. Before Tiffany had been Shanna, and before her, Colette. "Okay, she counts as a woman."

"Colette was also bright. She'd been to college and everything." He sounded smug, as if pleased he was going to win the argument.

Sabrina shifted until she was staring at him. "For all we know, Colette was a rocket scientist, but that's hardly the point. The woman, and I'll concede that she was a woman, was French. She barely spoke English, and I know for a fact you weren't the least bit interested in her brain. She was a lingerie model. Did you actually ever hold a conversation with her?"

"Sure."

Sabrina raised her eyebrows and waited. Cal had many flaws, but dishonesty wasn't one of them.

He sighed heavily. "Okay, it was a short conversation. What's your point?"

"I'm not sure I have one, aside from the usual. You're reasonably bright—"

He glared at her and she ignored him.

"Reasonably attractive—"

The glare became a scowl. She was also lying through her teeth. Calling Cal attractive was in the same league as describing New York City as a "large village."

"Somewhat articulate, very successful man who in the six years I've known you has yet to have anything resembling a normal long-term relationship. You're thirty-four. When are you going to settle down?"

"I've had long-term relationships."

"Taking your suits to the same dry cleaner for six or seven years doesn't count. Face it, boss, you're not actually interested in anything but the chase. You want them until you catch them, then you lose interest. Don't you ever think about something more than that?"

His brown eyes darkened. "My personal life is none of your business."

She picked up the bag containing Tiffany's parting

gift. "You make it my business," she said, no longer teasing.

He grunted. She'd heard enough of the sound to recognize it as a dismissal. He didn't want to talk about this anymore. There were times when she ignored the dismissive grunt, mostly because whatever they were talking about was important, but in this case, she let it go. Except when ending one of his relationships became her duty of the day, she really tried to stay out of his personal life. She admired Cal in many areas, but that wasn't one of them.

The limo pulled up to the west side high-rise in the Galleria district of Houston. Sabrina braced herself for the heat, slid across the seat and stepped out onto the sidewalk. She smiled at Martin, Cal's private driver, then followed her boss into the building that housed the corporate offices of Langtry Oil and Gas.

The business occupied the top three floors. While Cal headed directly for his suite in the southwest corner, Sabrina stopped to collect mail and chat with her secretary, Ada.

"What did you pick?" Ada asked, leaning forward and smiling. The fifty-something woman had worked for Langtry Oil and Gas for years. When Sabrina had been hired, she'd taken her time choosing an assistant of her own. Ada had a reputation for being a little grumpy and stubborn about doing things her own way, but she knew everyone in the business and had probably heard every whisper uttered in the company since the 1950s.

Sabrina handed her the Tiffany's bag. Ada raised her eyebrows. "Tiffany's for Tiffany? You know the subtlety is going to be lost on the girl."

"My thoughts exactly, but it was still fun."

As Ada opened the box and gazed at the bangle, Sabrina flipped through the mail. "What's the word on the street?" Sabrina asked.

"Number ten should be hitting oil tonight, tomorrow at the latest, even though the engineers say another three to four days of drilling. The only other piece of news is that the clerical supervisor is still having trouble keeping his hands to himself. He cornered another two employees by the copier. They're filing official complaints right now."

Sabrina looked up from the mail and frowned. "He's been warned. Cal doesn't tolerate that kind of behavior."

Ada slipped on the bracelet and shrugged. "Apparently he's bought into Cal's good ol' boy act and thinks the fact that the boss invited him to lunch once means they're best friends. I'm not sure. I'm just telling you what's happening."

"I appreciate it, Ada, and I'll tell Cal. He'll take care of it immediately."

Ada set the jewelry back in the box and sighed. "You did very well. She'll love it."

"That's the idea. To ease the pain of losing the man. Personally, I'd rather have the cash."

"Me, too. Tell Cal I'm ready to start our affair anytime he likes. Or we can skip the affair completely and just get right to the parting gift. I want something that can be easily returned. Remember that, Sabrina, when you're picking it out."

Sabrina laughed and rose to her feet. "I'll be sure and tell him, although I don't think he'll appreciate the fact that you're only interested in the gift and not the man himself. Cal considers himself something of a prize where women are concerned."

"Oh, he is. But we all know I'm old enough to be his mother. You, on the other hand—"

"Stop it, Ada. You know I'm not interested, either." She headed down the hall. "Talk to you later."

"You can't stay immune forever," Ada called after her.

"Oh, yes I can."

Sabrina ignored the elevator and climbed the elegant spiral staircase that led to the executive level. She'd offered Ada an office of her own up there, but her assistant claimed she had to stay down with the "little" people in order to hear all the good gossip.

As she climbed, Sabrina finished sorting through the mail. Nothing pressing, nothing she couldn't handle on her own. She reached her office, collected the messages Ada had left for her, then continued through to Cal's suite.

Floor-to-ceiling windows filled two walls of his huge office. Aside from the requisite desk big enough to land a Harrier jet on, a conference table and two leather sofa groups to encourage chatty conversations, he also had a big-screen television, every computer game known to man and a temperature-controlled wine "closet" that stored a few dozen of his favorites. There was a full kitchen and dining room beyond, an oversize bathroom complete with shower and Jacuzzi tub and a private elevator that led directly down to the parking garage.

As Sabrina approached the desk, she tried to ignore the view out the windows. Houston was about the flattest place on earth, and if she bothered to look, she could see forever. She'd watched thunderstorms roll in, perfect sunsets and, once, even a tornado dance across the land. In her opinion, Texas had too much weather. She missed Southern California, where the only way to tell the changing of the seasons was by the clothes being sold in the department stores.

Cal finished his call and motioned for her to take a seat across from his desk. She sank down into the leather chair and set Tiffany's parting gift on the chair next to hers.

Her boss met her gaze then looked away...almost as if he was embarrassed. How odd.

"Anything the matter?" she asked.

"No," he answered. "Just following up on something. It's...personal."

"Oh." Although she didn't know everything about Cal's life, she knew *almost* everything. And it had been a long time since he'd kept anything "personal" from her. At least she thought it had been.

"It's nothing important. Any of that for me?" he said, referring to the stack of mail in her hand and deliberately changing the subject. He wasn't the least bit subtle, she thought, and decided to let it go.

"Nothing I can't handle," she told him. "A few invitations."

He grimaced. "Charity functions."

"Of course."

"Just send a check."

She kept her smile hidden. If Cal wasn't "involved" with a woman, he got fairly reclusive. Society matrons loathed his dry spells, as he was often the life of their parties. It would take him a couple of months to find someone to replace Tiffany, then his social life would be off and running.

"I've heard from the number ten rig," he said. "The engineers figure another three to four days, but I think they're going to hit in the next twenty-four hours."

He never ceased to amaze her. Ada's contacts had

said the same thing. The difference was Cal made his assessment from his downtown office with nothing more than daily reports to guide him. Ada's source was an old oil man from way back who phoned her when they were getting close.

"What does Ada say?" he asked.

Cal watched as Sabrina tried to hide her annoyance at his question. She didn't like that he knew about her "source" in the office and would have preferred him to think she figured everything out on her own.

"The same," she admitted. "Within the day."

"Anything else I should know about?"

"The clerical supervisor is still having trouble keeping his hands to himself. A couple of staff members are filing official complaints."

Cal leaned back in his chair and rested his hands on the padded leather arms. "I can't say that I blame them. I hate it when this happens."

The coolly spoken words were enough to make Sabrina straighten. She reached for a pad of paper on the edge of his desk and grabbed a pen. "Go ahead."

"He's already been warned. Have Human Resources investigate the allegations and prepare the case, then fire him. Oh, I want them to promote from within this time—all the better if it's a woman so we can regain a little trust in that department—but tell them to be sure it's the best candidate, someone with a good record of employee interaction."

"That's it?"

He gazed at his personal assistant. Her wide blue eyes met his unblinkingly. "What did you expect? That I would call him out at dawn? Pistols at twenty paces?"

"I thought you'd at least threaten to beat him up."

Cal thought about the self-important young man who had been with the company less than a year. He'd been hired out of college, all cocky and convinced he was the next industry leader. Cal had put him in a supervisory position to season him. Obviously it hadn't worked.

"I would like nothing more than to show him what it was like to be physically intimidated by someone with the authority to hire and fire, not to mention someone physically stronger. However, letting him go under these circumstances is going to be plenty of punishment. He'll be left with a black mark on his employment record. So much for a rapid rise to success."

"Do you want to give him an exit interview?"

Cal grinned. "Let Ada do it."

Sabrina shook her head. "You are too cruel. That's perfect. He'll hate it."

"And Ada will adore it. I call that a win-win. Oh, and set up a department meeting with the clerical staff in the next few days. I want to talk to them myself. I don't approve of that kind of behavior. It's illegal and immoral. I want to reassure everyone that the situation is being corrected. Immediately."

Sabrina nodded as she took notes. She bent her head slightly, and the afternoon sunlight slipped through the window and caught in her short red hair—a layered cut falling just to the bottom of her collar. Her features were even, pleasant, if unremarkable. She had a nice smile, intelligent blue eyes and a figure that, after six years, was still something of a mystery to him. Despite the fact that she'd accompanied him on several working vacations, she always wore tailored clothing. Even her shorts-and-shirt sets had been proper and slightly loose. The only time he'd seen her in a bathing suit, it had been dark, and the shadows had prevented him from catching more than a glimpse of the occasional curve.

Not that he was overly interested in Sabrina's body. It was more male pride than desire. She was the perfect assistant—smart, attentive and not afraid to say what she thought. She had a gut instinct he'd come to rely upon, about people and situations. She didn't call attention to herself, and when he asked, she was willing to take care of his dirty work. The fact that she didn't turn him on was a plus. He didn't want the distraction and he couldn't afford to lose her.

He wondered what her reaction would be if he told her that the phone call she'd interrupted had been with an editor from *Prominence Magazine*. A letter had come to his house yesterday, telling him that he'd been named one of the world's most eligible bachelors by the magazine...and he'd been trying nicely to withdraw himself from such an ''award.'' Unfortunately, he'd hung up agreeing to do an interview instead. He could just imagine the way Sabrina's eyes would sparkle with amusement once she heard about his most recent ''honor.'' He would definitely wait to tell her.

They spent the next hour going through business. ''Don't forget the trip to Singapore at the end of September,'' he said. ''We're discussing the joint drilling venture.''

She continued to make notes. ''I remember. Maybe we can stop by Hong Kong on our way back and have some Chinese food. There's a lovely little restaurant there.'' She glanced at him, and her expression was innocence itself.

''I remember,'' he growled.

"Oh, Cal, you're not still sore that I beat you, are you?"

"I was never *sore* about anything. You got lucky in the fourth quarter."

"I was ahead the entire year. You've just conveniently forgotten that part." She grinned. "I'm also ahead this year."

He ignored her comment. For the past five years they'd had a bet on the stock market. On January first, he fronted them both ten thousand dollars to play the market. Whoever had the most money at the end of the year was the winner. The loser had to treat the winner to lunch anywhere the winner said. Last year, Sabrina had won and had claimed a taste for Chinese food...from Hong Kong.

"Actually, this year I've been thinking of Italian," she murmured.

"Rome?" he asked.

"Maybe Venice. I've never been to Venice."

"You've never been to Rome, either."

"I know, but Venice sounds so fun. All that water, those boats. Venetian glass."

She was already up twenty percent. It was his own fault. When they'd started their game, she'd insisted on a handicap. He wasn't allowed to invest in oil or gas stocks, the one area he was guaranteed a win. She, on the other hand, invested heavily in his own company. Last year that had been enough to push her over the top.

"I know a great Italian restaurant in New York."

The phone rang. She reached for it and grinned. "Don't even think about weaseling out of it," she said before picking up the receiver. "Mr. Langtry's office. This is Sabrina."

Cal didn't pay attention to the call. It hadn't come in on his private line, and Sabrina took care of most of his other business.

After a couple of minutes, she put the line on hold. "You'd better take this one," she said.

"Next year the rules are changing. Either I can invest in my industry or you can't, either." He put down the paper he'd been reading and glanced at her. "Otherwise— Sabrina, what's wrong?"

She'd gone pale. She didn't have much color in her face, anyway, but the little that was there had drained away, leaving her ashen.

"Is it Tracey?" he asked, knowing his older sister was usually responsible for any trauma in his life.

"No. It's your lawyer." She motioned to the phone. "You'd better talk to him."

Before he could ask her anything else, she rose and crossed the room, then let herself out. Cal frowned. He couldn't think of a single thing he and his lawyer had to discuss that would require privacy. Sabrina knew almost all of his secrets. It was part of her job.

"Jack," he said, when he'd picked up the receiver and released the hold button. "What's going on?"

"Are you sitting down, Cal?"

He didn't like the sound of that. "Get to the point, Jack. Whatever you said chased Sabrina from the room, and she's pretty unflappable."

"Okay. Do you remember a woman named Janice Thomas? You had a relationship with her back in college."

Cal frowned as the memory fell into place. "That was about twelve or thirteen years ago. Between college and grad school. We went out for a summer. What does that have to do with anything?"

"It seems she had a baby. A daughter. From what I've found out, when she discovered she was pregnant, she approached your parents. She wasn't interested in marriage as much as money. They agreed on a very tidy sum with the understanding that you would never know about the child. Unfortunately, Janice died in childbirth. The baby was given up for adoption. Her adoptive parents were killed in a car accident nearly a year ago. She's been living with an aunt in Ohio, an older lady who no longer wants responsibility for the girl. That's why I'm calling. I thought you'd want to know. If you don't take the girl, the aunt is going to make her a ward of the court."

Cal knew intellectually there weren't any fault lines in Houston, so the sudden tilting he felt couldn't be an earthquake. But that's how it seemed. As if his whole world had just been jolted from its axis.

"Cal, are you still there?" his attorney asked. "Did you hear me? You've got a twelve-year-old daughter."

A daughter? From Janice? The enormity of the information stunned him. Nothing made sense. A child? Him? No wonder Sabrina had left the room.

"I heard you, Jack." He'd heard, although he didn't have a damn clue as to what he was going to do now.

Two

"I don't know what to say," Cal told his attorney. He turned in his chair so he was facing the window, but he didn't even see the view. Instead, images of Janice filled his mind. He remembered her as being of average height and pretty. They'd met while interning for the same oil-and-gas firm one summer. "Are you sure about this? Why didn't she tell me she was pregnant?"

"Like I said, she was after money, not matrimony. I guess she knew about the trouble your parents had with Tracey and figured they would be willing to pay her off. One of the retired partners here at the firm prepared the paperwork, Cal. I've seen it. In fact, telling you this raises some issues regarding attorney-client privileges within the firm. But this is important enough that I'm willing to deal with any backlash. Janice was offered a sizable amount to keep quiet and stay away from you. If she hadn't died unexpectedly, she wouldn't have had to work again for life."

Nothing made sense. Cal tried to pick a rooftop outside and focus on it, but the task was too difficult. Janice had gotten pregnant? She'd gone to his parents instead of him? She hadn't wanted to get married, she'd just wanted the money?

"I don't want to believe any of this," he said, too stunned to be angry. "I tried to get in touch with her when I went back to college. She just disappeared. I thought she'd run off with someone else.''

A child. He couldn't imagine that being real. That one of those long summer nights had resulted in a new life.

Jack cleared his throat. ''Look, Cal, I'm your lawyer, not your conscience. You say the word and I'll pretend this conversation never happened. You don't know this kid from a rock and that doesn't have to change. Let the aunt turn her over to the state. It's probably better that way. The reports I have say she's been having problems. Poor adjustment in her new school, falling grades, antisocial behavior. Do you really want that kind of mess right now? Face it, your life is pretty damned good. Why change that?''

Cal knew Jack was just trying to do his job—which was to make his most wealthy client's life easier, however possible. Cal supposed there were many men who would simply walk away from this kind of information—he had a feeling he was going to wish he had. But he couldn't.

''If she lost her parents less than a year ago, I'm not surprised she's having trouble adjusting,'' Cal said. ''Everything's been taken away from her. She's living with an aunt who doesn't want her. She probably knows she's going to get thrown out any minute. These circumstances wouldn't make anyone look like a poster child for mental health.''

''You're right, of course,'' Jack said. ''I'm not the enemy here, I'm simply pointing out different options.''

''I know. I'm sorry,'' Cal said. ''This is impossible for me to believe. I can't help thinking I would have known if Janice was pregnant, but that, as Sabrina would gladly tell me, is male arrogance at its worst.''

''I understand. You're going to need some time to think about this. The aunt will keep her about two more weeks, so no decisions have to made today. There are a lot of different ways to play this one. I suspect with a little financial encouragement, the aunt might be willing to keep her longer. If you want, I can look into boarding schools. Or, as I already mentioned, she can go into foster care. You don't have to do anything if you don't want to.''

Cal felt as if he'd been blindsided by a tanker. He heard his attorney's words and knew he had plenty to think about, but one thing was certain. ''I'm not going to let her go to the state. If there's proof she's my daughter, then she's my responsibility.''

''Oh, there's proof. Your parents had her checked when she was born. There's never a hundred percent certainty, but within a reasonable doubt, she's yours.''

That was all Cal had to know. He'd done a lot of things in his life that he wasn't especially proud of, but he'd never walked away from his responsibilities. ''I have a few things to take care of. Sabrina or I will be in touch in the next day or so with the particulars. In the meantime, call the aunt back and tell her I'll be out to pick up my daughter before the end of the week.''

''Are you sure you want to do this?''

No, he wasn't sure he wanted to. He only knew he *had* to. ''If she's mine, Jack, I don't have a choice.''

His lawyer sighed. ''I figured as much. I'll let her know.''

''I'm going to New York to talk to my mother. If you have to get in touch with me, the office will know where I am.''

"Will do."

Cal was about to hang up the phone when he heard Jack call his name. "What?" he asked.

"Don't you want to know her name?"

The question shocked him. Giving the child a name made her more real—an actual person with an identity. "Yes."

"Anastasia Overton."

"Anastasia? What the hell kind of name is that for a twelve-year-old kid?" He shrugged. "I know you can't answer that one, either. Okay, Jack, I'll talk to you later." He hung up the phone.

Silence filled the room. Cal leaned back in his chair and swore. He pushed to his feet and stalked to the window. "What the hell is going on? How did this happen?"

He didn't even know what he was asking. Did he mean how had Janice gotten pregnant? That would be pretty easy to answer. Maybe he meant how had the pregnancy been kept from him? Or maybe how had his parents thought they could get away with keeping news of his own child from him?

But they had, a small voice whispered inside his head. For twelve years his mother had sat in silence. She'd sacrificed her own grandchild for the greater good. At least that's what she would tell him. He could already hear her voice.

The quiet got to him, and without thinking he turned back to his desk and hit a button beside his telephone. Less than thirty seconds later Sabrina stepped into the room.

Her usually animated face was strangely solemn. He half expected a crack, then realized that was never her style. She liked to banter and fight with him, but only on even terms. She would never attack him when he was vulnerable.

"How much did Jack tell you?" he asked.

Sabrina walked to one of the leather sofas and gracefully sank onto a cushion. He walked toward her and took a seat at the far end of the same sofa. He wanted to be close, but he found he couldn't face her. Odd, because Sabrina knew the worst there was to know about him. Knew it and didn't judge him. That was one of the reasons he kept her around.

"He said that you'd been involved with a young woman about thirteen years ago and she'd gotten pregnant, apparently on purpose. When you went off to grad school, she approached your parents, promising to stay out of your life if they paid her enough. They agreed. When the woman died in childbirth, the child was put up for adoption. She's now living in Ohio with an elderly aunt."

He faced front and braced his elbows on his knees, then clasped his hands together. "That about sums it up. Her name was Janice—the woman, not the kid." He glanced at her. "This is one of the bigger messes you've had to help me clean up. I guess you're going to be expecting a substantial raise this year."

She gave him a slight smile. "This isn't a mess. I would never think that. You didn't know about this. Jack told me he'd only found out about it a couple of days ago."

"You believe him?" He asked the question casually but suddenly found that her opinion mattered.

"Of course." She angled toward him. "Cal, you're nothing like your sister. Tracey is spoiled and willful. If this were her problem, she would have let the child go without giving him or her a second thought. You're not like that. If you'd known about your daughter from the beginning, you would have done the right thing, whether that meant marrying Janice or just providing for your child."

Her expression was earnest, her words sincere. He appreciated that. Jack had claimed not to be Cal's conscience, and Cal agreed. But there were times he wondered if that was actually part of Sabrina's job. Knowing that he was going to have to look her in the eye often influenced his behavior, and for the better.

"You're right. So thirteen years after the fact, I'm going to do the right thing. But first I'm going to New York to talk to my mother."

Sabrina raised her eyebrows. "I'm surprised."

"That I'm going to take my daughter or that I'm going to visit my mother."

"Both, although I'm more surprised about your mother. I don't remember you ever going to see her."

Cal grimaced. "We're not what you would call a close family. I think I've seen her twice since my father died, and that was nearly ten years ago. She wasn't the maternal type. Mother is very big on how things look rather than how they are. This situation proves that."

"Have you thought this through?" Sabrina asked.

He knew she wasn't asking about the visit. There was no reason to consider that. He needed information and his mother was the best source. After all, she and his father had been the ones to make the decision for him.

The shock was starting to fade, and he felt the first flicker of emotion since receiving Jack's phone call. It wasn't paternal pride at finding out he had offspring, or even curiosity at what his daughter would be like. Instead, what he felt was rage. Cold, dark rage. He told himself his parents had never considered his opinions or feelings before and he shouldn't be surprised they hadn't where Janice was concerned. Based on his thirty-four years as their son, nothing about their actions should shock him. Yet he was appalled at their complete disregard for his rights as a father and their callous disposal of their grandchild. As he had often thought in the past, he would have been better off being raised by wolves than Mr. and Mrs. Jefferson Langtry.

Sabrina leaned toward him. "We're talking about a growing child. She's nearly a teenager. Have you thought about what this is going to do to you and your life? If you really mean to take care of her, everything will have to change."

He stood up and paced in front of the sofa. "No, I haven't thought it through. I haven't had time. Right now I can barely grasp the concept of having a child. I haven't had a chance to internalize the information. But that doesn't matter. The girl exists and she's my responsibility. I'm not going to let her become a ward of the state. She didn't ask for her circumstances. She's a kid, and as far as she knows, no one in the world wants her. I might not be anyone's idea of a perfect father, but I'm not going to turn my back on her."

Sabrina smiled at him. "Every now and then you do something that reminds me why I like working for you."

"So it's not just about the money?"

"Not today."

He shoved his hands in his trouser pockets. "The good news is, once Tiffany finds out about my daughter, I won't have to worry about breaking up with her. She'll run so hard and fast, she'll leave skid marks."

"You don't know that. Maybe she would revel in the chance to show what she's made of."

Cal stopped pacing and stared down at Sabrina. Her blue gaze was steady. "I do know that," he told her. "I went out with her for nearly two months. While I don't know everything about her, I'm quite aware of her character. Besides, she's too young to be responsible for a twelve-year-old."

"But not too young to be dating that twelve-year-old's father?"

She asked the question with a straight face, but he saw the hint of a smile teasing at the corner of her mouth.

"You never give me a break," he complained.

"It's not in my job description. Besides, there are enough people thrilled to do that every chance they get."

"So you want to spend your time taking me down a notch or two?"

"No. It's not that personal. However, my job description *does* include telling you the truth, even when you don't want to hear it."

"It's your favorite part of the job," he grumbled.

"Sometimes." This time she did smile. "And I think there's a chance you could be wrong about Tiffany. She's not bright, but that doesn't mean she's heartless. She might surprise you."

Cal didn't want to be surprised. Even if Sabrina was right, it didn't matter. He wouldn't want someone like Tiffany near his daughter. Which was a pretty sad state of affairs, he told himself. He was willing to date and sleep with Tiffany, but he wouldn't want her hanging around his kid. So what had he seen in her in the first place?

He thought about her perfect twenty-year-old body and got a little of the answer, although he didn't like it. When had he gotten so damn shallow? Was this what he wanted *Prominence Magazine* to tell the world? Thank God he had Sabrina. He knew he could count on her. He also trusted her.

Sabrina glanced at her watch. "You could still catch a flight to New York this evening. You'll get in late, but that would allow you to see your mother tomorrow. I'm assuming you want this over as quickly as possible."

He nodded. "I want to get Anastasia in the next couple of days. She's living with an aunt, and the woman has made it clear to everyone that she's not interested in keeping the girl. That's a hell of a thing for a twelve-year-old to know."

Sabrina stood up and started toward his desk. "Let me see what I can do about getting you a seat. One night in New York, or two?"

"Make it two. I don't know how long I'll be with my mother, but I doubt we'll have a big family reunion. I already know our conversation is going to make me angry, and I'll need some time to get over it before going to Ohio. Oh, and book two seats, Sabrina. I want you to come with me."

His personal assistant looked at him. Wide blue eyes darkened slightly. "You want me to come with you while you talk to your mother?"

"Let's just say I haven't lost my temper with her yet, but I've come close. If anything was going to push me over the edge, this would be it."

"I'm not big enough to wrestle you into submission."

"I know, but one of your icy stares is usually enough to remind me to behave."

"Okay. I'll come, too. After all, I'm yours to command."

"Cheap talk. I command you to stop winning on the stock market."

She blinked slowly. "I'm sorry. Did you say something? I heard a faint buzzing, but no real words."

"Just as I thought. Selective hearing."

"I listen when you say something worth paying attention to."

He pointed at the phone. "Get us seats. If you promise to behave, I'll let you have the window."

"What a guy."

She picked up the phone on his desk and dialed from memory. While she talked with the airline, Cal crossed to the window and stared out. It was nearly dusk and lights were coming on all around him. He stared into the twilight and wondered about the little girl living somewhere north of here. What did she look like? He could barely remember Janice's face, although other images were clear to him. The sound of her laughter, the feel of her hands on his body.

There had been, he was willing to admit, an instant attraction between them. A fire that had burned hot and bright. He didn't remember asking her out, though. At the time, it had sort of seemed to happen on its own. Now, with the hindsight of age, experience and knowledge, he wondered if it had really been that casual. Had she set him up from the beginning, then engineered the entire relationship?

He remembered that the sex between them had been intense. With her claim of being on the pill, they hadn't worried about precautions. She'd always been eager and willing. At times, she'd been the one pulling him into bed. He remembered being flattered by her attentions and what he'd thought at the time was her insatiable desire for him. Now he realized she had just been making sure she got pregnant. He'd been a fool.

He remembered her tears when he'd left for graduate school, her promises to stay in touch. He remembered how he'd tried to call her, but her phone had been disconnected with no forwarding number. His letters had been returned without a forwarding address. It was as if she'd disappeared from the face of the earth. He supposed she had—after all, seven or eight months after they'd spent their summer together, she'd died.

He tried to feel regret for her loss, but he couldn't. He'd never known her. Whatever parts of herself she'd shown him had been designed to get him into her bed. Obviously he, too, had been born with the Langtry ability to completely screw up personal relationships.

How much had they offered her? What was a child worth these days? He pressed his hand against the cool glass and wondered how it was possible that his parents had performed this hideous deception. Then he reminded himself nothing they did should surprise him. With his family, he should know to expect anything...and nothing.

Three

Sabrina leaned back into the comfortable leather seat of the sleek limousine and told herself to relax. This wasn't her problem; she was simply an interested bystander. Cal wanted her along to provide moral support, nothing more. But the sensible words didn't stop her from clasping her hands together over and over.

She tried to distract herself from her nerves by staring out the window. As always, the city enchanted her. She'd never lived in Manhattan but had enjoyed her visits. She liked the contrasts of the city—the huge buildings, the large impersonal crowds, the street vendors who sold food and drinks on the corners and, after two days, recognized her and grinned as they asked if she would like her usual. She liked all the city had to offer culturally, she loved the theater and the restaurants. When she traveled with Cal, they stayed at beautiful hotels—as they had last night—but they didn't limit their culinary experiences to upscale, pretentious eateries. Instead, they found strange little places with unusual cuisine and often fabulous food. She liked the potential for adventure and the fact that no two visits were ever alike.

Under normal circumstances, she was usually thrilled to be in the city. Today, however, she would gladly give it all up to be back in the heat and humidity of Houston.

She didn't want to think about the upcoming visit, so she rolled down her window. It was a perfect New York spring day. Clear, warm but not muggy. The scent of blooming flowers occasionally overpowered the smell of exhaust. A burst of laughter caught her attention. She looked across to the sidewalk and saw a young father carrying his toddler son on his shoulders.

She swallowed. A child. She hadn't really allowed herself to think about children. She was still young and there was plenty of time. But children had always been a part of her future. She'd just assumed that one day she would have them. Cal was different. As far as she knew, he'd never even thought he would marry, let alone have a family. Here he was being presented with a half-grown kid. How on earth was he going to handle it?

She glanced at her boss. He stared straight ahead, and for once, his handsome face was unreadable. He didn't show his feelings easily, but over the years, she'd learned to read him. Until today. She knew he was in shock and he was angry. She couldn't blame him for either emotion. Bad enough to find out a former girlfriend had betrayed him in such a calculated way, but that information was made more horrible by the realization his own parents had joined the conspiracy.

Cal's father had died before she'd been hired and she'd never met his mother. She'd heard rumors and stories, mostly from Ada, about a cold society woman who put up with her husband's chronic philandering in order to keep her life-style intact. The marriage had been a business arrangement. One half had brought in land rich with oil; the other, technology, engineering know-how and a small infusion of cash. Separately the families had been struggling, together they formed an empire. An empire that, according to Ada, hadn't left any time for raising children. Cal and Tracey had been put into the custody of an ever-changing staff.

"What are you thinking?" Cal asked.

"That a twelve-year-old is going to change your life."

"I know."

"I don't think you realize how much. Children are a big responsibility. I remember helping Gram with my younger brother and sisters after our parents died. They were a handful."

He shrugged. "I don't have a choice. I'll learn what I have to. At least I want the girl. That's more than her aunt can say. That should count."

"It will." But would it be enough? Sabrina wasn't sure. After all, Cal wasn't into long-term commitments. His idea of a serious relationship was one that lasted two months. His record to date was ninety-three days. Still, a daughter was different from a girlfriend.

The limo pulled up in front of an East Side high-rise co-op. One of the uniformed doormen stepped to the curb and opened the door. Sabrina accepted his assistance from the vehicle, then waited for Cal to lead the way inside. She'd worked for him for several years and thought she'd grown used to their difference in background and wealth, but occasionally obvious signs of his family's impressive fortune intimidated her.

"I didn't call to say we were coming," she murmured as they stepped into the elegant foyer and walked to the elevators.

"I did. She's in this morning. She has a lunch appointment, but I told her this wouldn't take long."

Sabrina smoothed her hair, then tugged on the skirt of her hunter green silk suit. It was the most expensive work outfit she owned and she'd brought it deliberately. No doubt Mrs. Langtry would consider her beneath notice—after all, she was just the hired help. But she also figured she would need all the confidence-boosting she could get.

Instead of opening into a hallway, the elevator doors pulled back to reveal a huge living room. Marble floors and glass tables reflected the light from outside…light that flowed in through floor-to-ceiling windows. Unlike Cal's office view, this one didn't show a flat world, but instead stretched across Central Park, to the equally impressive buildings on the other side. The windows on her left looked south, and Sabrina realized Mrs. Langtry not only had a penthouse, but one on the corner.

Must be nice to be the other half, she thought, before the click of approaching heels caught her attention.

A very elegant, very beautiful older woman swept into the room. She had to be in her late fifties, but she looked substantially younger. Sleekly styled brown hair hung to her shoulders. She was thin, well-dressed and had the air of one born to society and money. Sabrina instantly felt dowdy. Her instinct was to take a step back in the presence of someone so different. Instead, she forced herself to square her shoulders and stand her ground.

"Good morning, Calhoun," his mother said. "You're looking well. Taller than I remember. You get that from your father, of course. The Langtrys are always tall. We'll talk in the morning room. It's this way." She motioned to a doorway on their right. "Your secretary can wait in the kitchen." Mrs. Langtry offered Sabrina a slight smile. "It's through there, dear.

Just past the dining room. Cook will get you some coffee and maybe a pastry.''

Before she could move, Sabrina felt Cal's hand on the small of her back. ''That won't be necessary, Mother. Sabrina isn't my secretary, she's my personal assistant. I don't have any secrets from her. She'll be joining us this morning.''

His mother's expression didn't change, but her nose twitched slightly as if she'd accidently inhaled an unpleasant odor. Sabrina resisted the urge to tell Cal she was more than happy to wait in the kitchen with Cook. For one thing, she would like to find out if Cook actually had a first name, and maybe even discover the gender of that person.

Nerves, she told herself. Okay, so she wasn't a Langtry, but she was an Innis, and while they weren't exactly top drawer, she'd graduated at the head of her class at UCLA. She was bright, funny and good at her job. So what if no one in her family was listed in the social registry?

''As you wish,'' Mrs. Langtry said, and led the way.

Sabrina stared at the woman's beige silk blouse. The fabric looked as if it was made from starlight, it was so smooth and flowing. Did the rich get fabric from a better class of silkworms? Did silk still come from worms? She would have to look that up when they got back to Texas.

The morning room was spacious and bright, with overstuffed sofas and a low table set with coffee service. Sabrina saw there were only two cups. Mrs. Langtry pushed a button on the wall. When a young woman in a black dress with a starched white apron appeared, she ordered a third cup and some pastries.

Cal motioned for Sabrina to sit on one sofa. She was

grateful when he settled next to her. She leaned close and whispered, "So do the afternoon and evening rooms get progressively bigger? I have no experience with this, you know. Back in California, we had one little old living room. It was good enough for the likes of us."

Cal grinned. "I'll fill you in on architecture of the rich on the way back to the hotel. It's pretty interesting."

"I'll bet."

She glanced up and saw Mrs. Langtry frowning. Sabrina doubted the older woman had heard any part of their conversation, so she must be unhappy with their obvious familiarity. She thought about telling Cal's mother that there was nothing going on between them, nor was that ever going to change, but she figured the woman wouldn't believe her, and even if she did, she would pretend not to care.

The maid returned with a third cup, then quietly left the room, closing the door behind her.

Mrs. Langtry poured coffee. She handed Cal his black, then looked expectantly at Sabrina. "Sugar? Cream?"

"Cream, please."

Mrs. Langtry complied, then held out the cup. When Sabrina took it, the older woman's attention turned back to her son. "I still think whatever you want to discuss would be better done in private."

"Sabrina knows it all, Mother. Well, not all. Obviously there are secrets even I'm not aware of, but those are the exception. After all, who do you think worked out the details of paying off Tracey's last husband?"

Mrs. Langtry's mouth pursed. "I see."

Sabrina resisted the urge to hunch down on the seat.

But she *had* been the one to take care of Tracey's problem. Cal's older sister had a bad habit of falling for men who were only interested in her money. She'd been married six times and had had an assortment of lovers, all of whom used her, taking what they could and leaving as soon as the funds dried up.

It was sad, she thought to herself. All this money and no one was happy. She remembered Ada's comments about Cal's mother being a cold witch. What no one could figure out was, had her husband fooled around because life was icy at home, or had his philandering caused the chill in the first place? Considering how they'd been raised, maybe it wasn't surprising the Langtry children hadn't found marital bliss, or even a decent relationship.

Cal set his cup on the coffee table. "Does the name Janice Thomas mean anything to you, Mother?"

"No." She took a sip. "Should it?"

"Yes, actually it should. Unless Tracey has a couple of kids that I don't know about, Janice was the mother of your only grandchild."

Mrs. Langtry drew in a deep breath. Her dark eyes, so like her son's, didn't waver. She took another sip, then nodded. "So you found out about the child. I suppose it was foolish to hope that unfortunate incident wouldn't come to light. Oh, well, you know about it now. No harm done."

Sabrina felt Cal start to burn. The heat of his anger singed her skin. She placed a hand on his forearm and gave a quick squeeze. His glance of thanks told her that he had been about to lose control.

"I don't know which comment to address first," he said, his voice low and controlled. "Your calling it an 'incident' or the statement of 'no harm done.' You played with lives, Mother. You kept information about a woman's pregnancy from me. You kept my child from me.''

She dismissed him with a wave. ''You don't know what you're talking about. You were what, twenty-two? Did you actually want to marry the little gold-digger? I don't think so. Your father and I knew exactly what had to be done. Janice Thomas didn't want to marry you, she wanted money. Under the circumstances, it was simpler to pay her off. I don't regret it for a moment, and you shouldn't, either. We were prepared to set her up for life. It's hardly our fault that she died.''

Sabrina knew that Cal's mother was cold, but she hadn't expected to feel the frost seeping into her body. She was stunned by the woman's callous words and had to consciously keep her mouth from hanging open.

''We are talking about my daughter and your grandchild. You had no right—''

The older woman set her coffee cup on the table and glared at him. ''We had every right,'' she said, cutting him off in midsentence. ''Your future was set, or it would have been if you'd ever bothered to settle down. You were going to run Langtry Oil and Gas. You barely knew the girl, so don't try to tell me you lost the love of your life. The truth is, you haven't thought of her once in the past thirteen years. All this righteous indignation over what? She was money-hungry trash. She got what she deserved.''

Cal set his teeth. ''I'll admit I didn't fall in love with Janice. I take issue with your comment that she got what she deserved, but that is not the point. I had a child and you kept that information from me. You let your own grandchild be adopted. I'll bet you didn't bother to keep track of her."

"No. Why should we? All this fuss. What's the point? The past is over. You wouldn't be interested in a child with a mother like Janice. I don't know how you found out about her, and I don't really care. If you want a child so much, marry someone suitable and have one. Stop chasing around with those young girls. You and your sister. Whatever did your father and I do to deserve such children?"

Cal rose to his feet. "Nothing, Mother. You two did nothing."

"Where are you going?"

"Why does it matter?"

"You're going to do something stupid, aren't you. Something with the child. This is why we didn't tell you about Janice all those years ago. You would have married the mother, or at least taken responsibility for the child. We saved you that, but you're not grateful. You don't understand. You've never understood."

"You're right, Mother. I don't understand. And yes, I'm going to go get *my* daughter, and I'm going to do my damnedest to be a good parent to her. But that's something *you* wouldn't understand."

Sabrina didn't remember standing, but suddenly she was at Cal's side and they were leaving the room, closing the door behind them. Mrs. Langtry continued talking, her words fading as they moved away. Sabrina was grateful. She didn't want to hear anything else. She was too shocked. Knowing that Cal's mother was a cold woman was very different from experiencing it firsthand.

They crossed the living room and waited in front of the elevator. Cal pushed the Down button.

"Cal?"

Both he and Sabrina turned toward the soft voice. Tracey Langtry stood in the shadows. She was a beautiful female version of her brother, or she had been at one time. The morning light was not kind, highlighting the lines on her face. Her life-style had not allowed her to age well, and she looked far older than her thirty-eight years.

Worn jeans hung on too-narrow hips.

"Cal, I need some money. I've used up my allowance."

Cal didn't look at her. Instead, he stared impatiently at the closed elevator doors as if willing them to open. "Who is he this time?"

"Oh, he's lovely. A race car driver. Very good, very young." She giggled. "Very nice in bed. I—" She hiccupped, then covered her mouth. "I like him a lot."

Sabrina realized the other woman was drunk, and it was barely ten in the morning. She considered herself fairly sophisticated, but this was too much. She took a step away from Tracey and toward Cal.

"There's a race and he needs the entry fee. Plus, traveling around gets so expensive. Please, Cal, just ten or twenty thousand. You won't even miss it."

He didn't answer. The elevator doors opened and he guided Sabrina inside, followed her and pushed the Down button. As the door closed, he didn't bother saying goodbye.

They reached street level and walked toward the limousine. Sabrina didn't think the silence between them was especially awkward, but she felt obligated to think of something to say. Something to tell Cal that she didn't judge him by his family. But she couldn't find any words. Not without making a difficult situation worse.

After they were settled in the car and he'd given the driver instructions to return them to their hotel, he finally looked at her. Something dark and painful lurked in his eyes.

"When I was a kid, I used to pretend that I'd been left on the doorstep by Gypsies and that one day they would come back to get me. At this point I would be grateful just to have been adopted. I'm not happy to have that gene pool floating around in my body. I could turn into one of them at any moment."

"If it was going to happen, it would have happened already. You're safe."

"You think so?" He turned toward the window. "I'm not so sure."

"Cal, you're a good man. If you were like them, you wouldn't care about your daughter. You would have let her go into foster homes or arranged boarding school. You're making an effort. That counts."

She wanted to tell him that she admired him. When she thought about all he'd been through as a child, of the horrible life he'd had, she was amazed that he'd turned out as well as he had. It was a testament to his character. Sometimes she forgot there was a real person behind the handsome playboy facade, then something like this came along and reminded her.

"I'm sorry you had to see that," he continued. "But I'm not sorry you were there. Lord only knows what I would have done to that woman if I'd been alone."

She wasn't sure if he was talking about his mother or Tracey, and realized he probably meant both of them. She didn't doubt that in a couple of days he would tell her to send his sister a check. Maybe not for the amount she'd requested, but for enough to tide her over until her next trust fund payment.

"Every family has dirty laundry. You'd be shocked if you knew some of my secrets."

He looked at her and smiled. "Yeah, right. You have secrets? What? That you went to bed without flossing twice all of last year?"

She glared at him. "They're more interesting than that."

"I doubt it. You are not the kind of woman who has deep, dark secrets. Don't worry, Sabrina, I'm not complaining. Far from it."

Before she could protest that she could be bad, too, if she wanted, he did the most extraordinary thing. He reached out and took her hand in his.

Sabrina blinked twice, then stared at their linked fingers. She and Cal often touched. A light brush of his arm against hers when they walked together. A teasing poke in her side if he thought she was being too stuffy. He'd hugged her a half dozen times or so over the course of their working relationship. But those had all been impersonal buddy-type contacts. This was personal.

She felt his heat and strength. His long fingers and broad palm dwarfed her hand, leaving her feeling incredibly feminine. A strange lethargy stole over her, and it was only when her chest started to get tight that she realized she'd stopped breathing.

She forced herself to draw in a deep breath, then release it. This wasn't happening. She glanced down and saw that it was. He was actually holding her hand. Then, as if he'd read her mind and realized what he was doing, he squeezed once and released her.

Sabrina sat next to him, feeling as if she'd just survived a force three tornado. Her entire body felt buffeted. Every cell was on alert, her skin tingled where it had been in contact with his, and if she allowed herself to notice, she would have to confess to a definite hint of dampness on her panties.

Danger! a voice in her head screamed. Danger! Danger! Do not do this to yourself!

She straightened and gave the voice her full attention. Every word was true. Cal Langtry was deadly to women everywhere. He was only ever interested in the chase. Once he'd caught his chosen prey, he lost interest and ended the relationship. She'd seen it happen countless times. Besides, they had a perfectly wonderful working relationship. She adored her job, she was well paid, and she wasn't a fool. Not only would she jeopardize everything if she started thinking of Cal as a man instead of her employer, she would be wishing after the moon. After all, she wasn't his type.

As painful as it was, she forced herself to remember a phone call she'd overheard nearly six years before. She'd been working for Cal all of two or three months and had been fighting a serious crush. It had been late and she'd entered his office unannounced.

He had his back to the door and didn't notice her in the shadows. She still didn't know who he'd been talking to and she didn't want to know. What she recalled most was that he'd been talking about her.

"Yes, my new assistant is working out great. I'm impressed with her." He'd paused to listen. "I did say 'her.' Sabrina is very much a woman."

She thought about how her heart had leapt in her chest and her knees had grown weak. Was it possible he'd been attracted to her, too?

"No, you've got it all wrong. She's perfect for me.

She's bright and too good for me to ever want to let her go. She's attractive enough so that no one is going to think she's a dog, but not pretty enough to interest me. It's great. No matter how closely we work together, Sabrina Innis will never be more than office equipment to me."

The words had laid her soul bare. She'd crept out silently and spent the rest of the night crying away her foolish dreams. In the cold light of dawn, she'd made a decision. She could continue to want what she could never have, or she could make the best of what was a wonderful job. With Cal she would make enough money to put her three siblings through college and provide for Gram. She would also be able to build a nest egg for herself. The position of Cal's assistant meant travel, all of which would be first class, a chance to meet interesting people and gain experiences she would never have otherwise. Did it matter that she didn't turn the man on?

In the end, common sense had won out over ego. She'd ruthlessly suppressed every hint of her crush until her wayward emotions fell into line. Now she could look at Cal and see him for the handsome bachelor he was without feeling anything but friendship. She'd bought gifts for his women and had made arrangements for romantic weekends away all without a twinge of jealousy or regret. So what had just happened?

Sabrina thought about all that had occurred in the past twenty-four hours. It must be the tension, she told herself. She hadn't slept much the previous night. Dealing with Cal's family was difficult for both of them. He'd reached out for comfort and she'd happened to be the closest person. She'd reacted because he was a good-looking man and she'd been living like a nun.

Wayward hormones and close proximity. Nothing else. She didn't have any romantic feelings for the man. How could she? She knew the worst about him. She still liked him, but she sure wasn't fooled by his charming personality. Cal Langtry might be an incredible catch, but he had flaws, just like everyone else.

The limo pulled up in front of the hotel. She looked over at her boss. "What do you want to do?"

"There's no point in staying here. Let's change the flights and go to Ohio this afternoon. I'll call Jack and have him notify the aunt. If I can, I want to get my daughter as soon as possible."

Four

The town was a three-hour drive from the airport. Cal slowed at the intersection. There were only two other cars in sight and both of them were at least ten years old. Although he'd traveled to many unusual places, he'd always lived in large cities—Houston, Dallas, New York for a short time. In the back of his mind, he'd wondered what it would be like to live in a place where everyone knew everyone else.

"Follow this street about a mile," Sabrina said, consulting the handwritten directions Jack, his attorney, had provided them. "Then turn right. Oster Street. There should be a stop sign."

There were small business on both sides of what was obviously the main road. A diner, a barber shop, a closed five-and-dime. He was about to say it didn't look as bad as Jack had made it out to be when he noticed the peeling paint on most of the buildings. Some of the windows were boarded up. The farther he drove into town and away from the highway, the more run-down everything seemed.

He turned right where Sabrina indicated. Commercial and retail areas gave way to houses. He saw a lot of broken or missing fences, cars up on blocks. Side yards contained clotheslines with drying garments flapping in the brisk breeze. Porches sagged, yards were overgrown with weeds. They passed a block with five houses for sale, four of which had signs proclaiming the price had been reduced.

"This place is dying," he said.

"I know. It's sad. Jack said the main factory closed and there's no employment. A lot of people have already gone, and those who stayed are having trouble earning an income. In a couple of years, there won't be anything left."

Their rental car was a plain General Motors four-door sedan, nothing fancy. But it was relatively new and seemed out of place on the narrow street. "I'm glad we didn't take a limo."

"I agree. Turn right at the stop sign." Sabrina rolled down her window and took a breath. "I feel badly for these people. You can smell the poverty." She shivered. "What's that saying? 'Been there, done that, bought the T-shirt.' I don't want to go back."

Cal frowned. "You told me that you grew up without a lot of money, but things were never this desperate, were they?"

"Not really. We didn't have extra spending money, but we got by. After my folks died and we moved in with my grandmother, we had a few months that were pretty difficult, before the social security kicked in. Then it wasn't so bad. Besides, Gram was a hoot to live with. I remember her standing at the stove fixing macaroni and cheese. We had it about three times a week because it was cheap and all us kids liked it. Anyway, she would stir in that orange powder stuff, look at me and say, 'Sabrina Innis, being poor sucks. You make sure you do better.'" Sabrina laughed. "She was wonderful."

"Yeah." He thought about his half dozen meetings with Sabrina's grandmother. The feisty old lady was opinionated, but charming as hell. "Why don't we have her out to visit soon?"

"I'd like that. Thanks. But we're going to have to wait. She's planning a summer trip to Alaska. I know she's going on a ten-day cruise, and after that, she and her friends are taking the train through the state."

Cal knew exactly who was paying for Gram's vacation. "You're generous with her."

"She was good to me and I love her. I want her to be happy."

"You also listened to her statement that being poor sucked. Is that why you took the job with me?"

When Sabrina had graduated from UCLA, she'd had four serious job offers with Fortune 500 companies. Cal had been recruiting for his firm as well, and when he'd first interviewed Sabrina, he'd realized she could be a great assistant for him. As the job didn't come with room for advancement or a lot of corporate exposure, he'd sweetened the pot with promises of travel and a generous starting salary.

Sabrina chuckled. "Are you asking if I only want you for your money? Cal, it's not like you to be insecure."

"I'm being serious."

"Oh, serious. That's different." Her blue eyes twinkled. "Okay, the money was a large part of it. I wanted to help Gram out and I had three younger siblings heading for college. But that wasn't the only reason I took the job. I knew I would be giving up some things, but working for you offered the opportunity to travel, to learn about a major corporation from the top down. There was also the issue of moving to Houston. I was ready to be on my own, and getting out of Los Angeles made that possible."

He had the oddest urge to ask her if she had any regrets. Regrets about not taking the other jobs. He told himself he was reading too much into her words. At times the job was difficult, but he knew Sabrina enjoyed her work. If she didn't, she would have moved on a long time ago.

"Were you heartbroken when you realized I wasn't a Texas cowboy?" he asked, his voice teasing.

"Oddly enough, no. I already have to put up with you calling me 'little lady' every couple of days. I don't need to add the smell of cow manure to the equation. You're a good ol' boy, Cal. That's plenty. Oh, this should be the street. The address is 2123. There it is, on the left."

He parked their rental car and turned off the engine, but made no effort to get out. For a moment he could only stare at the small house.

The walkway was cracked and overgrown with weeds. Any grass had long since died. There were missing panes in the windows, and those remaining were too filthy to see through. The screen door hung on the top hinge only.

"This can't be right," he muttered. "Jack said Anastasia's adoptive parents were middle class. Not rich, but nothing like this."

"These aren't her parents," Sabrina reminded him. "The woman she lives with is an aunt, maybe not even that closely related. Jack wasn't sure."

"My daughter can't live here," he said, then swore. "How could my parents have let this happen?"

"You're going to fix it. That's what matters, Cal. You came as soon as you found out about her."

Her. My daughter. The words were spoken, but they had no meaning. On the other side of that door was a child he'd never known about. A flesh-and-blood person with hopes, dreams and feelings. What was she going to say when she saw him?

He pushed away the question because he didn't have an answer, then got out of the car. Sabrina did the same and came around to his side.

He gave her a brief smile. "Thanks for coming with me. I would have hated to do this alone."

"No problem. I'm happy to help." For once she didn't tease and he was glad.

He studied her, the short, layered red hair, the familiar face, the concerned expression. She wore tailored khaki slacks and a cream blouse. As always she was sensible and in control. He admired those qualities in Sabrina, and right now, he was depending on them.

He nodded toward the house. "Let's go."

He led the way to the front door and knocked. There was nearly a minute of silence that left Cal wondering if they had the wrong place or if no one was home. Then the door opened. A woman in her late fifties or early sixties stared up at him.

"What do you want?" she asked, her voice throaty and her tone annoyed. "I ain't gonna buy anything, so don't bother trying to sell me whatever you've got."

"Mrs. Sellis?" Cal inquired politely. "I'm Cal Langtry. I believe my attorney spoke to you on the phone. I'm here about my daughter."

The woman was small, not much over five feet, and very thin. Her clothes were worn and stained. Gray streaks highlighted her short, dark hair. She looked Cal up and down, then grinned, exposing yellowed teeth and three empty spaces.

"So you decided you wanted the brat, did you? I can't figure out why, but you'll save me the trouble of filling out paperwork, so that's something. You'd best come in.''

She held open the screen door. Cal led the way inside. The living room was small and dark, with tattered drapes hanging over the dirty windows. Pizza cartons and empty potato chip bags littered the floor. The center of the sofa looked as if it had been hit by a bomb, with springs poking up through a large hole in the dark brown tweed fabric and bits of stuffing burping out onto the other cushions.

The woman shuffled to a rocking chair in front of a new television and sat down. The tray table next to her contained a pack of cigarettes and an overflowing ashtray. She took a cigarette and lit it, then inhaled.

"You're early," she said. "We wasn't expecting you until the end of the week."

Cal glanced at Sabrina. Mrs. Sellis hadn't invited them to sit down, and neither of them made a move to settle on their own. For one thing, the couch looked filthy and uncomfortable. For another, he wanted to bolt.

"I finished my business more quickly than I expected," he said. "Is Anastasia here?"

"Of course she's here. Where else would the girl be? She's twelve. I don't let her run around on her own. She might not be blood kin, but I've done good by her. She's had a place to stay and food to eat. There are some who wouldn't have been so kind."

Sabrina touched his arm. He knew what she was trying to tell him—that this woman had probably done the best she could. Maybe it wasn't her fault she lived in such a poor house. Of course, she could have bothered with picking up the trash at least.

Mrs. Sellis took a deep puff on her cigarette and

coughed. When she'd caught her breath, she yelled, "Anastasia, get your stuff and get on out here, girl." She turned her attention back to Cal. "She'll be right along. Did you bring the check?"

Cal stared at her. "What check?"

"Figures." She stubbed out the cigarette. "I'm not handing the girl over to the likes of you for free, you know. Her fool parents up and died without a penny to their names. Her daddy had just changed jobs, so there weren't any life insurance yet. I took the girl in because I'm family—" She frowned. "After a fact. They did adopt her. Well, I did the right thing and it's been nearly a year. I get a little something from social security, but it's not enough."

Mrs. Sellis pushed herself to her feet. "She's nothing but a trial, I don't mind telling you that. Sassy mouth on her, always talking back. She won't do her school-work. Grades falling, getting in trouble at school. She ran away a couple of times." The woman glanced around her living room. "From here, if you can believe it."

"Mrs. Sellis, the social security check would have adequately provided for Anastasia's needs," Sabrina said quietly. "Mr. Langtry's attorney didn't mention that any reimbursement sum had been discussed."

Cal recognized Sabrina's tactic instantly. They were going to play good cop, bad cop. He wanted to protest that he usually got to be the bad cop, but in this case, it was probably better that he come off as the good guy. After all, his daughter might be eavesdropping on the conversation.

Suddenly reminded of the girl's presence in the house, he glanced around the small room. To the left was a tiny kitchen with an even smaller eating area. To the right was a single door. It would lead to a hallway, he thought, or maybe just to the only bedroom in the house. Again he was stunned that his child had been living under these circumstances. If only he'd known sooner.

"You his wife?" the woman asked.

"No, Mr. Langtry's personal assistant."

Mrs. Sellis cackled. "Is that what they call it these days. Oh, my. An assistant."

Cal's temper flared. "Name your amount. I will be happy to write you a check. In return you'll sign a paper saying you never want to have anything to do with the girl again."

"Well, that's the truth, I'll tell you. If I never see her again, it'll be too soon. That one's nothing but trouble." Her dark eyes glittered. "Of course, she's your own flesh and blood and that should make a difference."

The anger increased. He didn't like this woman. At first, he had felt some compassion for her circumstances, but now he didn't give a damn. "I would like to see my daughter."

"I know, I know. Anastasia, get out here, girl. I mean now!" She turned from the door. "What kind of a name is that, I ask you. Anastasia. Like she's someone important, instead of a skinny brat with a nose for trouble."

The door opened. Cal stared, his heart pounding as he waited to catch his first glimpse of his daughter. Someone stepped into the room. A young preteen, caught in that awkward stage between childhood and physical maturity.

She was about five foot five or six, just a little shorter than Sabrina, with large dark eyes hidden behind glasses. Her hair hung to the middle of her back. He registered those facts before getting caught up in horror at how painfully thin she was. Her too-small, worn T-shirt clung to her, exposing her bony shoulders and rib cage. Her cheeks were sunken and her mouth pinched. Jeans hung off her hips.

There was dirt on her face and hands, and her hair was greasy. He couldn't tell if she was pretty or not. He couldn't do anything but stare in shock.

"What the hell have you been doing to her?" Cal demanded in a roar. "There are laws against this kind of neglect."

The girl's eyes widened. "I'm not going to the state home," she shrieked. "I'll run away and you'll never find me! I swear, I'll die first."

She made a quick move as if to run out the door. Cal stepped forward to block her. "You're not going to the state home," he said quickly. "I'm not from the government. I'm your father."

He said the words without thinking, then the meaning sank in. Her father. This was his child. Not at all what he'd pictured, but no less his.

Sabrina felt as if she were caught up in a movie. Everyone was reacting to a script, but she didn't have a copy of today's dialogue. She stared at the girl standing—shaking—in front of them and her heart went out to the child. What terrible pain had she endured in the past year? No wonder she'd been a discipline problem. From the looks of things, Mrs. Sellis wasn't overflowing with compassion and concern.

The girl watched Cal warily, as if deciding whether or not to trust him. He took another step toward her. Sabrina wanted to warn him to take things slowly. After all, if she was having this much trouble absorbing what was happening, Anastasia would be suffering with the same problem.

But she couldn't get it together enough to speak. She was too stunned by Anastasia's appearance and this tiny house that smelled of neglect and poverty.

Cal reached out to touch his daughter's cheek. She spun away and glared at him. "You're not my father," she spat. "You're just the bastard who knocked up my mother. Go to hell."

With that, she raced for the bedroom and slammed the door behind her. Sabrina flinched at the sound. Cal looked as if he'd been sucker punched. Only Mrs. Sellis didn't react.

"I told you she was difficult. So, about the check. I think eight thousand ought to cover it."

"If you think—" Cal began, then visibly took control of himself.

"Excuse us," Sabrina said, then moved close to him, took his arm and pulled him into the kitchen. "Cal, look at me."

"That woman," he growled. "She's been starving her. That kid hasn't eaten in days. Longer. Don't try to tell me she's got an eating disorder. This isn't about trying to be thin enough. We're talking about neglect and possibly emotional abuse. I can't believe—"

He stopped talking and ran his hand through his hair. "Dammit, Sabrina, did you hear what my own kid said to me?"

"I know, but you can't take it personally. She's scared. She doesn't know you from a rock, and here you are, ready to take her away."

"Anything would be better than this place."

"She doesn't know that. This is all she knows right now. Okay, it's horrible and she hates it, but at least it's familiar.'' She gazed at her boss. ''What do you want to do?''

''I want to get my kid out of here.''

She thought for a moment. ''Why don't you talk with Mrs. Sellis and I'll collect Anastasia. I think I'm less of an emotional button for her right now. As far as how she was treated, you can call Jack when we're in Houston and let him take care of it.''

Cal swore, then pulled Sabrina close and rested his chin on her head. ''Thanks. I wouldn't be able to get through this without you. I'd want to tear that old lady apart, limb by limb.''

Sabrina ignored the fluttering in her chest and the heat from Cal's body. ''You wouldn't like prison, Cal. I don't think you'd do well there.''

''Probably not.'' He took a step back, then shrugged. ''She's going to come around, isn't she?''

She knew he meant his daughter. ''She's been through a lot and it's going to take some time, but sure, she'll come around. You're going to be a great dad.''

She spoke with more confidence than she felt. While she didn't doubt Cal's abilities, she was concerned about Anastasia. She'd suffered tremendously, and she'd had to do it alone. That kind of experience could leave a person scarred for life.

She and Cal went back into the living room. Mrs. Sellis watched them, her dark eyes glowing with greed. Sabrina ignored her and crossed to the closed door. She hesitated, almost afraid of what she would find on the other side, then drew a breath and turned the handle.

The bedroom was tiny, dark and even more dirty than the living room. Sabrina didn't want to think about what might be living under the bed. Clothes were scattered all over. There were dirty plates, glasses, torn magazines and dirt everywhere. Anastasia lay curled up on the bed, with her back to the door. Her shoulders shook, but she didn't make a sound.

Sabrina stared at her and tried to decide the best way to handle the situation. Her instinct was to offer the girl comfort, but her gut told her that was wrong. Right now Anastasia was scared and angry. Compassion would be viewed as weakness. She decided to go for logic.

"Boy, were you stupid," she said, her tone conversational.

That got the hoped-for response. The girl stopped crying.

"Talk about blowing a perfect setup. Look at this place. It's disgusting. I know you hate it here."

"No, I don't" came the defiant response.

"Oh, so that's why you ran away a couple of times. And now this basically nice guy shows up, a guy who is, by the way, your father. He just found out about you and he wants to take care of you. Instead of saying thanks or even hi, you call him a bastard and run out of the room. Like I said, not really bright. I guess you want to go to that state home, huh?"

Anastasia rolled over and glared at her. "No, I don't. I won't go there. I swear, I'll die first."

Sabrina shrugged. "You want to stay with Mrs. Sellis?"

Anastasia wiped the tears from her face. The moisture smeared the dirt there. "She hates me. She only wants the money the government sends." Full lips trembled. "I want to go home."

Sabrina's chest tightened. She knew exactly what the girl meant. She wanted her old life back—the one where her adoptive parents were still alive and she was allowed to live in blissful ignorance about the tragedies of life.

"I know," Sabrina told her. "Unfortunately, no one can make that happen. But living with your dad might not be so bad. You could at least try it."

Anastasia glared at her. "Who are you? His wife?"

It was the second time that day she'd been asked the question. "No, I work for him."

"Oh, the secretary." The dismissal was clear.

"No, the personal assistant. I'm the one who makes his life run smoothly. If you're smart, you'll realize I'll have the same power over your life. I'm not so bad, kid. I have two sisters and a brother, all three younger than me, so I'm on to you. You can't scam me. I know this isn't going to mean anything now, but I'm more than willing to be your friend." She held up her hand. "Don't say something you're going to regret later."

Anastasia just glared.

Sabrina smiled brightly. "So what's it going to be? You want to throw a tantrum or two and stay here? I think Mrs. Sellis is serious about sending you away. Or you can take a chance on your dad and come along. Houston is kinda hot in the summer, but it's nice." She looked around the room. "Nicer than here. With a little luck you might be happy there."

"If I was lucky, I would still have my parents." Anastasia sat up. "Why does he care about what happens to me?"

Sabrina assumed the "he" in question was Cal. "Because he's your father. He wants to take responsibility for you. Foolishly, I'll bet he even wants to care about you."

The girl's mouth twisted as if there was no way she was going to believe that.

"It's up to you. You coming or not?"

Anastasia drew in a deep breath, then rose to her feet. "I guess."

They were standing pretty close. Sabrina noted the dull cast of her skin and the unwashed smell of her body. This kid needed someone to care about her, and she was willing to bet Cal was the man for the job. It wasn't going to be easy, but it would be worth it in the end.

She motioned to the room. "Do you have a suitcase?"

Anastasia stared at her as if she'd grown another head. "I'm not going to bring anything from here. I want to forget I ever saw this place." She headed for the door, then changed her mind. "Wait." She bent down, drew a tattered shoe box out from under the bed, then clutched it to her chest. "I'm ready."

Sabrina stared at her dirty face and thought her heart was going to break. She knew better than to ask about a doll or other toy. Anastasia wouldn't have any. Obviously taking clothes would be a waste of time. They would all have to be thrown out, anyway. She swallowed the lump forming at the back of her throat and led the way to the door.

They entered the living room. Mrs. Sellis stood holding a check and looking stunned.

"Let's go," Cal said, and motioned for them to leave.

Sabrina touched Anastasia's thin arm. "Do you want a minute to say goodbye?"

Anastasia didn't even glance at the woman who had taken care of her for the past year. Instead she marched outside without once looking back. "Is that it?" she asked, pointing to the rental car.

"Yes."

She walked toward it, then climbed into the back seat and slammed the door shut. She sat still, staring straight ahead.

"My lawyer will be in touch," Cal told Mrs. Sellis.

"You tell him to call me and I'll sign whatever you say." The woman smiled. "She's a fine girl. You're going to be happy you took her."

Cal let the screen door slam into place. He put his hand on the small of Sabrina's back and ushered her toward the car.

"A fine girl?" she questioned. "So how big was the check?"

"Ten."

"Thousand?" She went on without waiting for a response. "She doesn't deserve anything but a trip from social services. No wonder she suddenly thinks Anastasia is a prize."

"Anastasia is my daughter, and the old woman *has* custody of her. It would have taken time to get custody if she didn't hand it over. And I wasn't going to leave Anastasia there another minute."

They paused by the car door. Cal glanced at her. "She called me a bastard."

"She was upset."

"She's only twelve. How does she know language like that?"

"Cal, they say words like that on television."

"I guess. It's just…"

"She's not what you were expecting."

"There's an understatement," he muttered.

"You're the one who said she'd been through a lot," Sabrina said, reminding him of his words.

He grunted in response, indicating he wanted to

change the subject. She wasn't going to let him get away with that.

"Either you understand or you don't," she said. "You had to know this was going to be difficult. If you're not up to taking responsibility for her, decide now. She's not a puppy you can return to the breeder if it doesn't work out. She's a human being, with feelings and hopes and dreams. Right now she's an ill-tempered bratty girl who has not only lost her parents but lived with that woman for the past year. It's going to take a lot of time and love to help her heal. It may never happen. Are you prepared to take that chance?"

Cal stared back at the small house, at the weed-filled lawn and the crooked screen door. "You don't think much of me, do you?"

"Actually I think a lot of you. However, I'm not sure you're prepared to deal with this reality."

He wanted to tell her she was wrong, but he knew better. Everything Sabrina said was the truth. He had thought Anastasia would be different. At least cleaner. But that wasn't her fault. Was he willing to be responsible?

"She's my child," he said. "If I'd known about her, I would have taken care of her when she was born. I'm still willing to make sure she's all right. I don't expect it to be perfect."

"Or even easy."

He glanced at the sullen child in the car. "It's not going to be easy. I've already figured that part out."

He walked around to open Sabrina's door, then returned to the driver's side and stepped into the car.

"Did Sabrina tell you I live in Houston?" he asked as he fastened his seat belt.

Anastasia didn't acknowledge he'd spoken. He

checked in the rearview mirror. Her gaze remained fixed straight ahead.

"We'll be flying there. Have you ever been on a plane?"

She shrugged faintly. "No, but it's no big deal. Even dorks can fly."

He swallowed the flash of irritation and the sharp retort that followed. "I know this is hard," he said, gentling his voice. "I just found out about you yesterday, so we're both kind of in shock. I want—" He paused, not sure what he did want. "I want you to be happy with me. It will take some time for us to get to know each other, but that won't be so bad."

She didn't respond.

He glanced at Sabrina, who gave him an encouraging smile. "I'm sorry about your adoptive parents," he told his daughter.

She raised her head and glared at him. Even in the reflection of the rearview mirror, he felt the intensity in her gaze.

"They're not my adoptive parents," she said loudly. "They're my real parents. Get it? Real. As in the only parents I've ever had and the only ones I want. I don't want you. You're not my father, you're some, some sperm donor. I don't want to be here. I don't want to go to Houston. I don't want to talk to you or anyone, so just leave me alone."

Cal turned in his seat in time to see her fold in on herself. She wrapped her arms around her chest and rocked back and forth. Sobs caught in her throat like hiccups.

He was furious at what she'd said, surprisingly hurt by her assessment of his value in her life, uncomfortable and confused by her tears. So far, parenting was a bitch.

Sabrina reached out and touched Anastasia's head. The girl jerked back. "Leave me alone," she muttered.

His assistant shrugged. "You're not going to take her back to that woman, so let's just drive to the airport. We can figure this all out later."

Cal started the engine. They drove in silence. Eventually Anastasia's tears slowed. She curled up on the seat, and by the time they'd traveled about ten miles down the interstate, she was asleep.

He looked at Sabrina. "Thank you," he said.

"For what?"

"For just being with me. I couldn't have done this without you."

She smiled. "That's why you pay me the big bucks, boss."

He knew she was more than an employee. Their relationship had always been largely undefined. Sometimes strictly business, sometimes more like friends. He didn't care what people called it as long as she stayed right where she was.

Five

The flight to Houston was going to take about three hours, and they'd already been in the air for nearly two. Cal leaned back in his seat and tried to relax, but he couldn't. Again and again his attention strayed to the seat across the aisle where Anastasia lay curled up, asleep.

"You can't solve all the world's problems today," Sabrina said, repeating a phrase he often used on her.

"I hate it when you throw my words back in my face," he muttered. "And I know it's true. I can't. But what about her?"

The first-class section of the aircraft had two seats on either side of the aisle. Sabrina had taken the single seat across from the two together, but Anastasia had wanted to switch. Obviously she wasn't interested in sitting next to her father.

Cal tried not to take her actions personally. The kid had known about him only a few days, and they'd been in each other's company for less than five hours. She was alone and scared, and the past year of her life had been hell. It made sense that she would do her best to protect herself against what she saw as threats to her safety. But telling himself was one thing, while believing it was another.

He looked at the child he'd fathered, at her dirty hair and thin face. He wondered what Anastasia thought of her first plane trip, of the amenities of first class. Then he reminded himself she had nothing to compare any of it to. At least he knew she'd enjoyed the food. She'd gobbled her dinner with a haste that had made him wince.

"What are you thinking?" Sabrina asked.

He forced himself to relax a little. "I was wondering how long it had been since the kid had eaten."

"She was enthusiastic about her meal," Sabrina agreed.

She glanced down at her list and crossed off another item. Since the meal service had ended, Sabrina had been on the in-flight phone, making arrangements and ordering things for his daughter. He was, Cal realized, pitifully unprepared for the arrival of a child into his life. Just thinking about the professional but impersonal decorations in the guest room made him wince.

"No," Sabrina said quietly. "You're not allowed to think that you made a mistake."

"I wasn't thinking that."

"Something close." She laid her hand on top of his forearm. "You're not to blame for Anastasia being so unhappy, nor are the circumstances of her life your responsibility. You never knew about her. If you had, you would have done something. As soon as you found out, you took measures to get her."

Her touch comforted him. He looked at his daughter. "She's not exactly what I imagined."

"Remember what you told Jack. That she's been through a terrible year. No one would thrive living with Mrs. Sellis. Add the loss of her parents and you have a recipe for disaster."

"Are you saying there's nothing to be done? That she'll never come around?"

Sabrina shook her head. "Of course not. But she's going to need a lot of time and love. If there isn't some progress in the first couple of months, counseling might not be a bad idea."

Cal grunted. Counseling he could handle, but the love part... What was that? To the best of his knowledge, his parents had never loved him or Tracey. He knew he'd never really loved anyone, and none of the women in his life had ever felt that emotion for him. Love. Maybe it was all a fantasy.

It was his fault. He'd pictured the meeting between him and his daughter as something of a cross between a television sitcom and the musical *Annie*. The thought of his daughter being someone like Anastasia had never occurred to him. Of course he probably wasn't what she wanted, either.

He looked at his daughter. Curled up in the wide seat, she seemed so small and painfully thin. "I don't know what to do with her. I don't know what to say."

"Say that. Tell her you're just as confused as she is. When a child loses his or her parents, everything in the world changes. One minute you're secure and innocent in your belief that life as you know it will go on forever. The next minute, that innocence is ripped away. It's a painful process. Kids aren't sure they can ever risk trusting anyone again. What if they do and that person goes away?" She tapped her pen against the paper resting on her tray and shrugged. "You can get over the pain, but I doubt anyone who has been through that ever forgets."

"How old were you when you lost your parents?"

"Fourteen. So a couple of years older than Anastasia. I also had the advantage of my brother and sisters around me. Gram stepped right in to take care of us, so we never had to move. That was something, but it wasn't enough. That was the hardest thing I've ever been through. Your daughter had it much harder than I did. Try to remember that.''

''The next time she calls me a bastard?''

''Maybe it will help.''

A faint smile tugged at the corners of her mouth. Cal studied Sabrina's face. So familiar, so comforting. He'd grown used to asking her advice and listening to her words. She was his sounding board, his trusted adviser, his friend and sometimes his conscience.

''All right, little lady,'' he drawled, knowing she hated to be called that. ''I'll take what you said into consideration.''

''Toad.'' She removed her hand from his arm.

''It occurs to me,'' he began, ''that you're the one with the expertise in this area.''

She turned toward him and shook her head. ''Don't even think about it,'' she warned. ''I mean it, Cal. For one thing, Anastasia isn't a mess to be tidied. For another, she's your daughter and you have to take the time to get to know her, not to mention letting her get to know you. That's important. I know it will be hard, but you have to struggle through this on your own.''

He resisted the urge to whine that he didn't want to. Mostly because he knew she was right. ''I don't know how to do this.''

''I'll help,'' she promised. Her eyebrows pulled together in a frown. ''I know it's none of my business and you don't have to answer if you don't want to, but what was it like for you, when you were growing up?''

He shrugged. ''Different from what you remember, I'm sure. We had a big house in River Oaks,'' he said, naming the exclusive area of Houston. ''My father traveled a lot. My mother had charities and luncheons all the time. There was a staff, although we never kept anyone for too long. For reasons I'll never understand, my mother always hired young, attractive women to work in the house. My father didn't believe the rules of fidelity applied to him, so he took advantage of the 'landscaping,' as he used to call them. Mother would find out and fire the women. Anyone lasting three months was considered a family retainer."

Sabrina's blue eyes darkened. "Cal, that's horrible. You knew about your father and what he was doing?"

"Sure. He bragged about it. Kept telling me that I was just like him." Cal stiffened in his seat, then had to consciously force himself to relax. "I swore I would be different. That's why I only date one woman at a time. No commitment, but complete monogamy."

She angled toward him and rested the side of her head against the seat back. "I shouldn't have asked."

"It's not a problem. You probably need to know this. In case I get weird with Anastasia or something. My parents were never much interested in us unless they needed to parade us out, or wanted to be seen at a sporting event or recital. I was the serious kid, did well in school, that kind of thing. Tracey was born wild. She's four years older, and I think I was about ten the first time she ran away. By the time she was fifteen, she'd already had an abortion. She didn't get into drugs much, but she loves her liquor."

"I'm sorry," she said.

"Nothing to be sorry for. I survived. Look at where the company is now. We're earning four times what we did when my father was still alive."

"But that doesn't make up for the past."

She saw too much. In an effort to distract her, or

maybe because he needed the connection, he took her free hand in his.

Her skin was smooth, her nails short and neatly filed. She didn't resist the contact, nor did she encourage him by responding. He was, he knew, getting close to a line he'd never crossed with her. For one thing, he refused to be his father, who had been forever after the hired help. For another, he respected Sabrina too much to play games with her.

But this wasn't a game. Maybe it was Anastasia. Maybe it was that they'd been working together for so long. Whatever the reason, lately he'd been feeling that he needed Sabrina. Thank the Lord she was happy in her work. He would never get through this without her.

"Think there's a class in parenting I can take?" he asked.

She laughed. "Sure, but it's going to be about dealing with newborns. Most people learn to be a parent while their offspring learn to be kids. You're jumping in the middle. Give yourself a break, Cal, and don't expect perfection the first time."

"I don't expect anything close to that. I just don't want to screw up too badly."

"I promise to point out any gross errors."

"I bet you can't wait. You always get a kick out of telling me I'm wrong."

"I know." She sighed. "One would think I would get tired of that, what with you giving me so many opportunities."

The insult sunk in and he squeezed her fingers. Not enough to hurt, but enough to get her attention. "You, little lady, are being disrespectful."

"You, Mr. John Wayne wannabe, earned it."

Her smile was contagious. Cal felt some of his tension ease. He'd never failed at anything in his life. There was no reason to think he couldn't have a good relationship with his daughter.

Sabrina freed her hand and tucked her short hair behind her ear. In the soft overhead light, she looked younger than thirty. While she wasn't his type, she was pretty enough. Her mind was razor sharp and a constant challenge. She was funny, sensitive and easy to be with.

"So why aren't you married?" he asked.

Sabrina stared at him. "Excuse me?"

"You've been working for me for over six years and I've never once heard you mention having a man in your life. Why?"

"I don't have time."

"That's a crock. You have evenings and weekends off, not to mention four weeks of vacation a year."

"Cal! Be serious. I'm usually with you until you leave for your dinner date, which means seven or seven-thirty. A lot of times, I still have more work to do. We travel constantly. More weekends than not I'm in the office, or following you around some event. As for vacation, last year I took two long weekends to visit my family. According to Ada, I've accrued about ninety-seven vacation days."

Had he really been working her that much? "You could have said something."

"I'm not complaining, I'm stating facts. The truth is, I haven't minded. I knew what the job would be like when I took it. For the past few years, career has been more important to me. When that changes, I'll do something about it."

"Just don't take those ninety-seven days all at once.

Everything would fall apart." And he would miss her. Cal pushed that thought away.

"I won't, I promise."

"So there's no one who's caught your eye? No young executive or engineer in the company?"

She covered her face with her hands, then let her arms drop back to her sides. "Do not even think about fixing me up with one of your executives. I told you, it hasn't been important to me."

He studied her for a minute, then snapped his fingers. "Someone broke your heart," he announced, pleased he'd figured out the mystery. On the heels of pleasure came concern. "Who was he?"

She glared at him. "I'm not even going to ask how you figured that out. Okay, yes, there was this guy, but it was a long time ago and it's not really important."

He leaned toward her. "Tell Uncle Cal everything."

She took a deep breath. "I was in college and I fell for this guy. He was very popular and handsome. You know the cliché. I couldn't figure out why he would want to date me, but he did. Anyway, we were together nearly two years. I thought we were going to get married. He thought he would use me to get his grades up high enough to get into a great law school. And he did. He left for Harvard and never once got in touch with me again."

She told the story easily, as if it didn't matter. Enough time had passed that maybe it didn't. But Cal thought he saw tension in her body.

"Do you still miss him?"

She looked at him as if he were insane. "Of course not. He was a jerk."

"But he broke your heart."

"Let's just say he made it difficult for me to trust easily."

He wanted to ask her if she trusted him. Not that it mattered, he told himself. They had a relationship based on the fact that she was his employee, nothing more.

"Don't worry about me," she said. "For now, this works."

He didn't like the sound of that. "And when it doesn't work?"

She raised her eyebrows. "You didn't expect me to stick around forever, did you?"

Actually, he'd never thought about her leaving. "So you're going to leave me for a man. That's just like a woman."

"It's just like a man to say 'just like a woman' when he's trying to get his way." She gave him a quick smile. "Don't worry, Cal. I have no plans to leave anytime soon. I'll be around to help you with your daughter."

He'd nearly forgotten. Cal turned and looked at the sleeping girl. She was much quieter when she was asleep and he found he liked that. It gave him time to think and try to figure out what on earth he was supposed to do with her now that he had her.

"You can't leave," Cal said, his voice low but frantic.

Sabrina raised her eyes toward the heavens and planted her hands on her hips. "I can't stay here forever. Face it, you're going to be alone with your daughter eventually. Why not get it over with now? In time it will get easier."

He glanced over his shoulder. They stood in the liv-

ing room of his penthouse condo. Anastasia was checking out the rest of the place. "Nothing about the girl
is easy. I don't understand why you won't make an
exception to your rule. This is important. It's not just
about what's easier for me, either. Anastasia would feel
better with a woman around."

She groaned. Damn the man, he was probably right
about that. Because she wasn't emotionally involved in
the situation, it was easier for her to deal with the preteen. So far all of Anastasia's smart-mouthed comments had been directed at her father.

But move in? Here? "I can't," she said.

"You won't. There's a difference." He glared at her.
"There are four bedrooms, so don't tell me this is a
privacy issue. I'm not asking for anything permanent,
just for a few weeks until things are settled."

She crossed to the window and pulled open the
blinds. The city stretched out below, all twinkling
lights and endless night sky. Everything Cal said made
sense. It wasn't forever. Why was she resisting so
hard?

Sabrina folded her arms across her chest and sighed.
Because, she thought. Because there was an inherent
risk involved with moving in. Warning bells went off
every time she thought about it. Over the past few
years, Cal had mentioned that life would be easier if
she were closer. But she'd resisted. She hadn't wanted
to be a part of his social life, and she refused to live
at his place while he was entertaining one of his
women. Going to dinner was one thing, trying not to
hear them doing the wild thing was another.

But Anastasia wasn't one of his women. He *had* just
ended things with Tiffany, so he wouldn't get involved
with anyone else for a few months. Maybe longer. So

that wasn't a problem. Still, the warning bells told her too-close quarters would be a risk. If only she could figure out why.

"We need you, Sabrina."

She'd always been a sucker for being needed. Cal knew that, too, and he was using it against her. She could feel herself weakening. He made matters worse by coming up behind her and placing his hands on her shoulders.

"Please?"

His voice was low and seductive. A blend of masculine charm and Texas accent. When he was like that, he was irresistible. Thank goodness he didn't know.

"All right," she told him. "I'll move in for a few weeks. But don't think I'm going to take responsibility for your daughter. You need to get to know each other, and that's not going to happen if you thrust her on me all the time. The quicker you bond with her, the better for both of you. For me, too."

Cal swept her up in a bear hug. She felt the length of his hard body against hers and wondered at the quirk of nature that made him so incredibly attractive to her, while he barely noticed she was female.

"Thank you," he said, spinning her around once before setting her on the floor. "You won't be sorry."

"Why do I doubt that?"

"No one knows but you. So now what?"

"Now I head home to get some sleep and pack up my stuff. You get to work bonding with your daughter."

"She's not interested in bonding. She hates me."

Sabrina shook her head. "She's alone and she's scared. Think of a wild animal lashing out, only instead of using teeth and claws, she uses words. It's the only way she knows to protect herself.''

Cal grunted.

Ah, the signal to change the subject. This time, because she'd said as much as she wanted to, she didn't pursue the matter. She could see that Cal understood what she was telling him, even if he didn't want to.

"The things I ordered from the plane will be here shortly," she reminded him. "Take them to her."

"A bribe?"

"Think of it as a peace offering." She crossed to the door, grabbing her purse on the way. "I'll see you in the morning. Don't worry, you'll survive."

"I doubt it." He opened the door and stared out forlornly. "Get here early, okay?"

"I promise."

She met his gaze. He looked lost and abandoned. She had the strangest urge to offer some kind of comfort. But the only thing that came to mind was a hug, and maybe a kiss. Ridiculous, she told herself. Cal didn't think of her that way, and she'd taught herself to ignore the fact that he was a good-looking man. She must be tired if she was forgetting that particularly hard-won lesson.

"I'll see you in the morning," she said, and started for the elevator.

Cal hovered outside his daughter's room. He wanted to talk to her, but he didn't know what to say. First of all, he wanted to apologize for the sterile decorating. He hadn't expected the room to be occupied by a twelve-year-old. Then he wanted to explain that he was nervous, too, but that they might be able to at least be friends.

He knocked on the closed door. "Anastasia?"

"Go away."

At least she was a straightforward communicator, he told himself as he retreated. He paced in the living room, not sure if he should try knocking again, or maybe just barge in. After all, the door didn't lock. But he hated to invade her privacy, and he wasn't sure what he should say. If Sabrina were here, she would know what to do.

He glanced at his watch and saw that she wouldn't have had time to get home yet. Damn. He would have to wait to call her. Then he would—

The doorbell rang. He sprinted toward it, incredibly grateful for the interruption. Maybe Sabrina had come back to rescue him.

But instead of his assistant, he found a young man in the hallway. He carried a half dozen shopping bags all bearing the logo of a local department store.

"Delivery for Mr. Langtry," the man said. "Here you are, sir."

Cal tipped him and collected the packages. Sabrina had ordered clothes and other things for Anastasia. Cal grinned. Now he had an excuse to talk to his daughter.

He headed down the hall and knocked on her door.

"I already said 'go away.' Do I have to spell it out on the door for you to understand?"

"Not really." Cal shifted the bags to one hand and opened her door.

Anastasia had been lying on the bed. She shrieked and jumped to her feet. "I could have been getting dressed."

That hadn't occurred to Cal, then he realized that wasn't possible. "You don't have any other clothes."

"That's not the point."

"If you'd been polite enough to let me in, opening the door wouldn't have been an issue."

"I didn't want to see you. Besides, why should I be polite?"

"Because you're in my home and I expect common courtesy from you."

She glowered but didn't answer.

Cal set the bags on the floor. She stared at them with undisguised curiosity but didn't mention them. Good. A little anticipation might soften her up.

"How are you doing?" he asked.

She shrugged.

She'd showered. Her hair was damp, her face clean, although her clothes were still filthy and hanging on her. Her glasses slid down her nose and she pushed them up.

"I didn't have enough time to get the room ready," he said. "Why don't you think about how you'd like to change it?" He motioned to the plain dresser topped only with a glass sculpture that was more blob than person, although the decorator had assured him it was stunningly representational of true love. "Maybe some different furniture and wallpaper or paint."

Anastasia shrugged again as if it was of no importance to her. "There's no TV," she complained. "Or books or magazines. Don't you read? Or does your assistant read to you?"

Irritation flared and he carefully banked the feelings. She was just a child, and as Sabrina had reminded him, she was lashing out so that he wouldn't know she was scared.

"There are a lot of books and magazines in my study," he said calmly. "Many of them are about business, so I don't think you'll find them interesting. However, we can go to a bookstore in the next couple of days so you can get some reading material." He remembered the packages. "Sabrina may have ordered some when she called about clothes."

He picked up the bags and set them on the bed. "She called from the plane so these things could be delivered tonight. I don't know if they'll fit, but they're a start. I guess a shopping trip is in order. I'll put it on the schedule."

Anastasia stared at the bags. "Those are for me?"

"Sure."

Mistrustful brown eyes turned in his direction. "All of that, or just some of it?"

"All of it. I wouldn't have brought it in to you if it wasn't yours."

She bit her lower lip. "I don't have any money. What do you want for them?"

People talked about their hearts breaking. He'd never understood the concept or felt anything close to a snap. But at that moment, with his daughter staring longingly at the packages but not daring to step closer to them, he felt something. If not a break, then certainly a major crack.

She was only twelve. She shouldn't understand the concept of having to offer something to get something. Gifts and surprises should be a part of her life. There had been surprises, he thought grimly, but only the tragic kind.

He crossed to her and placed his hand on her shoulder. She froze. He half expected her to shrug him off, but she stood there, trembling like a cornered kitten. "Anastasia, I want you to have these things because I want to take care of you and I want you to be happy.

You aren't expected to pay for them except to say thank you."

She glanced at the bags, then at him. "Thank you." The word was a whisper.

She moved to the bed and dumped the contents of the first bag on the plain navy comforter. Cal saw what looked like shorts and T-shirts, some underwear and something that might have been pajamas. Working quickly, she upended the other bags. There were sandals, bathing suits, a robe, several books, a portable cassette player and tapes, and in the last bag, a large stuffed bear.

Anastasia fingered the soft-looking fur, then shoved it away. "I'm not a kid," she said defiantly. "I don't play with stuff like that."

Considering how stubborn his daughter was, he figured she must like the bear most of all, but she wouldn't dare show that for fear it would be taken away. Dammit, what had she endured in the past year?

He pushed the clothes aside and sat on the bed. She remained standing. "I know this is hard for you," he told her. "You don't know me, this is an unfamiliar place. We're talking about a lot of scary stuff."

"I'm not scared."

"Really? In your position, I would be terrified. Probably peeing on the rug like a puppy."

That earned him a slight smile, which she quickly suppressed.

"I've never been a father before."

"Duh."

He ignored her. "But I was a kid. Some would tell you I was a kid for longer than I should have been. The point is, I know you're nervous and concerned about what's going to happen. I want to try and make you happy, but you have to try, too, Anastasia. We need to work on this together.''

Her chin raised slightly. ''I'm not going to be happy ever again.''

''I see. You know, being happy doesn't mean you won't still love your adoptive parents. They wouldn't want you to spend your whole life mourning them.''

''What do you know about them?'' she demanded. ''You don't know anything. And they're not my *adoptive* parents, they're my real family. You're not my father, you'll never be my father. I had the best father in the world, and no one will ever be better than him.''

Tears spilled out of her eyes and slid down her cheeks.

''I know that's true,'' he said, ignoring the jab of pain in his chest. ''He will always be exactly perfect. I accept that. But that doesn't change the fact that you live with me now, and I am your biological parent. You're my daughter.''

''No!'' She wiped her face, but more tears fell. ''No. You didn't want me before so I don't care that you want me now.''

''I didn't know about you before. I just found out about you yesterday.''

A sob shook her. She shuddered. ''You should have known. If I was really your daughter, you should have known about me. You should have come and taken me away. But you d-didn't.''

She ran into the bathroom and slammed the door shut behind her. He could hear the sound of her crying. He ached for her—no one should ever be that unhappy.

He stood up and crossed to the door, but this one he left closed. He had no right to intrude on her pain. Instead he walked out of the room and went into his study. After pouring out a stiff drink of Scotch, he took a sip and wondered what he was supposed to do now. He wasn't prepared to be responsible for his daughter. He didn't know how to be a father. He was probably doing everything wrong. He'd never loved a child or even been loved *as* a child. He was completely in the dark on this one.

He took another drink of the Scotch and decided it would be a great night to get drunk.

Six

Sabrina walked to her window and glanced out. The view wasn't nearly as nice as it was at Cal's condo, but she didn't mind. The lush garden, overgrown into a tangle of fragrant flowers and vines, reminded her of a New Orleans courtyard. She rented a two-bedroom guest house on a stunning estate in the River Oaks district of Houston. The place had its own single car garage, and the owners of the property were gone more than they were home. The location put her only a couple of miles from Cal's place and the office. Best of all, the rent was reasonable. Ada had found it for her when she, Sabrina, had first moved to Houston. Back then, every dime had been important, and she'd been thrilled with both the floor plan and the price.

Now, although she could easily afford to pay three times as much in rent, she didn't want to move. She'd grown used to the neighborhood and being close to everything. She liked the quiet of the estate...at least she had until tonight. For reasons she couldn't understand, this evening the quiet made her restless.

Or maybe it was something else, she mused as she moved from the window to the sofa and thought about sitting down. She could read. Although she wasn't someone who watched a lot of television, there was always her collection of movies. Or maybe a nice hot bath. The larger of the two bedrooms had a beautiful bathroom, complete with separate stall shower and oversize Jacuzzi tub.

None of the suggestions sounded right. She strolled into the kitchen and pulled open the refrigerator. Nothing inside called to her. There was some triple chocolate ice cream in the freezer. She grabbed a spoon, took a mouthful, then set the pint carton back on the shelf. No, she wasn't hungry. She was looking, but for what?

Maybe the past couple of days had upset her more than she'd realized. Learning that Cal had a daughter was one thing, but actually meeting the child was another. Anastasia. While Sabrina understood the girl's fears and her need to protect herself by lashing out, she didn't envy Cal the job of "taming" the angry child. It was going to take a lot of love and patience. She'd seen her boss take as much time as was necessary to close a deal, but he'd never been as willing to go the distance with people. Certainly not with the women in his life. But Anastasia was his daughter and that would make all the difference in the world. He might just surprise them.

She returned to the living room and sank onto the sofa. What was he doing right now? she wondered. It was after ten, so Anastasia was probably asleep. Did she like the clothes? Sabrina had had to guess on the sizes, but she was pretty sure she'd gotten them right. They would go shopping in the next couple of days and pick up some other things for her. After all, she'd arrived with nothing.

Sabrina thought about the tattered clothes the girl had worn, the dirt on her face and how thin she was. No child should have to live like that, with both physical and emotional neglect. It wasn't right. She pulled her knees up to her chest and reminded herself that things were going to be different. Anastasia had family now. Cal might not be anyone's idea of a traditional parent, but he wouldn't turn his back on his responsibilities.

The restlessness grew. Sabrina frowned. She was going to be spending the next couple of weeks at Cal's condo. If she knew her boss—and she did—he would try to talk her into staying longer. So this was her last night alone for a while. She should enjoy it.

Yet, for once, the solitude didn't heal her or comfort her. Something was off, something she couldn't put her finger on.

Maybe if she called a friend, she thought as she rose to her feet and crossed to the phone. It wasn't too late. She could call one of her sisters on the West Coast, where it was two hours earlier. Or she could—

Like most revelations, when this one occurred it was both startling and unpleasant. Sabrina stopped in the middle of the floor and turned slowly in place. She took in the neatly decorated room with its pine furniture, cream sofa and contrasting Colonial blue wing chair. She'd collected the artwork herself, buying a piece at a time, some from galleries, some from estate sales. A few were framed posters. Her collection of movies and books filled a cabinet in the corner. Each of the other rooms in the house had been decorated with the same care and attention to detail.

It was a facade. A pleasant, pretty facade that hid the truth from everyone—even herself. But reality had just hit her upside the head and there was no escaping the truth.

She didn't have a life. She hadn't had one for years. At least not one of her own. There were no friends she could call in Houston. Oh, she had some acquaintances from work, women she went to lunch with occasionally. She was still close to her sisters, but college kept them busy and they had their studies and their friends. Phone calls every two weeks weren't a substitute for actual emotional intimacy.

Everything she had, everything she thought and everything she was had been linked with Cal. She had become her job with nothing left over for herself.

She returned to the sofa and sank down. When had it happened? She shook her head, already knowing the answer to that one. During her first interview, Cal had warned her that he demanded long hours and plenty of travel. She'd been thrilled with both the opportunity and the starting salary.

Cal had been an answer to her prayers. Between salary, raises, bonuses and stock options it had taken less than four years to fund everyone's college plans. Two of her siblings had opted for the more inexpensive state colleges, while the youngest had been offered a partial scholarship to Stanford. Once they were taken care of, Sabrina bought Gram a condo by the ocean, one close to her friends and the social activities she adored. Now everyone had been taken care of, even Sabrina herself. She'd been investing her money. She'd learned a lot working for Cal and now had a nice nest egg. *And no plans for a future,* she thought.

The truth was she would never have a life as long as she worked for Cal. He was like the sun. If you stared at it, the light was so bright, you couldn't see anything else. As long as she was around him, she wouldn't be able to deal with what she wanted. The job had been perfect...at the time. But times had changed. Maybe she should plan to move on.

She ignored the voice inside that cried out she didn't

really want to leave. This was comfortable and familiar. There had to be a compromise. She ignored the vague feeling of apprehension. Change was never easy, but sometimes it was the right thing to do.

She walked into the guest bedroom and moved to the desk against the far wall. There, in a file, were the letters she'd received over the past few months. Letters from headhunters telling her about jobs available to someone like her. She'd been recruited before but hadn't been interested. If it was time to move on, then these companies were her ticket out.

She stared at the file. Did she really want to leave Cal? Did she have a choice? She'd gone as far as she could go professionally. There would be more money, but that wasn't enough anymore. The other reality she tried to ignore but couldn't was that the longer she stayed, the more she was at risk emotionally. Cal was the kind of man she could fall for big time. She'd gotten over her initial crush, which was good. But now she actually knew him and liked him, despite his flaws. If she got emotionally attached to him, then what? He wouldn't be interested in her—he'd made that very clear. She wouldn't want to settle for an affair, and he didn't do anything else. Besides, Cal only wanted what he couldn't have. He was interested in the chase. She was already a part of his life, so there wouldn't be much of a hunt.

She carried the folder to the kitchen and set it on the table. It was definitely time, maybe past time, for her to do something. Before she left for Cal's in the morning, she would make a few calls and see what was available. She wasn't ready to make a decision, but it wouldn't hurt to ask around.

It was nearly midnight. Cal was well and truly on his way to being drunk. The buzz had become a roar, but it wasn't going to be enough to let him forget.

He rose from his desk and moved into the hallway. There, he stared at the closed door, behind which slept his daughter. Son of a bitch, what was he doing with a kid? He didn't know the first thing about raising a child. She was almost a teenager, which made matters worse. Plus, she hated the sight of him. How was he supposed to make this work?

Bracing himself for the tirade if she was still awake, he slowly opened her door. He paused before stepping into the darkness.

Enough light spilled in from the hallway to allow him to see the bed. Anastasia lay on her side, curled toward him. Her brown hair had dried from her shower and lay across the pillow. She'd exchanged her dirty clothes for a new nightgown. There was something dark by her midsection. He stepped closer and saw she clutched the teddy bear to her chest. One arm was tightly wrapped around the toy, as if even in sleep she was afraid someone would take it away.

In the shadows, she appeared small and defenseless. He could see the faint tracks of her tears, and his heart went out to her. He was worried about her, about what was going to happen, and he was a grown-up who was secure in his life. Imagine what this twelve-year-old must be feeling. Everything she'd known had disappeared. The people who had raised her were gone, the woman she'd been thrust upon had made it clear she was unwelcome. Now a stranger had swept her up into an unfamiliar world. No wonder she lashed out.

Unfamiliar emotions filled him. There was a tightness in his chest, along with a burning at the back of his throat. He wanted to go to her and hold her close, promising that everything would be fine. But the words held no meaning. Everything wasn't going to be fine and they both knew it.

He wished Sabrina was with him. She could explain this to both of them. She always knew the right thing to say. Thank God she was moving in tomorrow morning—otherwise they would never make it.

As he watched this child who was his daughter, he tried to figure out who she looked like. He saw traces of Janice in her—also flashes of himself. Her mouthiness and temper, for example. Pure Langtry.

Janice. He backed out of the room and returned to his study. He didn't want to think about her, but he didn't have a choice. He couldn't change the past, but he had to learn to deal with it. A woman he'd trusted had betrayed him in a significant way. She'd used him to get pregnant so she could go after the family's money.

He sank back into his chair and poured another Scotch. So he'd been a fool. He wasn't the first man to be taken in by a woman and he wouldn't be the last. So what?

But it was more than that, he thought grimly. He should have known, or at least guessed there was a problem. How could he have been so stupid? Why hadn't he seen through her?

Maybe he hadn't wanted to, he admitted. She'd been young and pretty and very willing. At that age, sex had been more important than feelings. Janice had encouraged him, making love wherever and whenever he wanted. Looking back, he realized she'd been far more experienced than he. He hadn't been looking for anything long term, but he hadn't expected betrayal, either.

He didn't understand her motives and he never would, although it was safer to think about her than to remember his parents and their part in what had happened. He wasn't ready to rage at his mother for her thoughtless interference. Damn the woman.

"Why are you surprised?" he asked aloud, before downing half his drink. "These are the Langtrys, after all."

They were all sharks. Even him. He didn't want to be like them, but sometimes he was. Blood would tell and all that. They were the reason he avoided commitment and love. He wasn't even sure love existed. He'd never seen it at home and wasn't sure it could survive in the world. So where did that leave Anastasia? With a father who didn't know the first thing about loving a child.

Maybe, he thought as the alcohol gripped his brain and made the edges of the room start to blur, just maybe she would have been better off as a ward of the state.

He'd forgotten that sunlight could hurt so much. Cal blinked as he stepped out of his bedroom. There were skylights in the hallway. He winced and squinted, but it didn't help. The pounding in his head only increased. He had no one but himself to blame—after all, he knew the potential effects of too much alcohol. He'd been trying to bury his pain, but it was back in full force and this time with nasty physical manifestations.

Coffee, he thought desperately. He needed coffee.

He headed for the kitchen, only to stop in the doorway when he saw Anastasia sitting at the table in the corner. She'd poured herself a bowl of cereal and was in the process of opening a milk carton. She'd brushed her hair back from her face and secured it in a braid. A red T-shirt and matching shorts hung loosely on her slender body, but they were an improvement over the rags she'd had on the previous day. She was pale and skinny, but she looked a lot better. She was, he realized with some trepidation, going to be a pretty young lady.

She glanced up and saw him. "You look terrible." Her voice was loud and the tone was exactly high enough to start a series of jackhammers going in his head.

"I know," he muttered. "I feel terrible. I just need some coffee, then I'll be fine."

"Why do adults drink coffee?" she asked. "It tastes gross. It's all dark and yucky. You should try milk. It's much better."

His stomach lurched at the thought of him swallowing milk at that moment in time. "Maybe later," he said as he hurried to the cupboard and fumbled for a filter. There was a can of grounds in the refrigerator. After measuring out enough for a pot and filling the reservoir with water, he flipped the switch, then prayed it wouldn't take to long to brew. In preparation, he got down a mug and waited impatiently. At least he'd had the good sense to get a coffeemaker that would allow him to pour a cup before the pot was full.

Anastasia took a bite of her cereal and chewed. The crunching sounded overloud to him. He tried not to wince.

"There's not much food here," she said when she'd swallowed. "Just this cereal and milk. You don't eat here often, do you?"

"No." He made the mistake of shaking his head and had to swallow a groan. The pounding by his temples was rhythmic—keeping time with his heartbeat. A nice steady *thunk, thunk, thunk,* at about sixty beats per minute. He felt clammy and his skin was one size too small. He didn't want to think about the army currently camping on his tongue.

"Mrs. Sellis didn't like me to eat too much. She said food was expensive. Is it going to be like that here?"

There was a note of worry in her voice. Cal forced himself to ignore his symptoms and look at his daughter. Before he could answer, she squared her shoulders and shrugged.

"I don't give a damn," she said. "I don't need you, you know. I can run away from this place, just like I ran away from hers."

"Tell you what, kid," he said, forcing himself to remain calm, knowing giving into irritation would only make the hangover worse. "You stop swearing and I'll make sure you get enough to eat. We'll go to the grocery store as soon as Sabrina arrives."

She eyed him mistrustfully. He had the feeling he was being measured against some invisible benchmark, and he knew in his gut he was going to come up short.

He waited for her to ask the inevitable "And if I don't?" for which he had no answer. But she didn't. She shrugged again, as if to say it didn't matter to her, then shoved a spoonful of cereal into her mouth.

Cal inhaled the scent of coffee and realized the pot was full enough for him to pour a cup. He'd just taken his first healing sip when Sabrina breezed into the kitchen.

"'Morning, all," she called in bright, cheery, migraine-inducing voice. She looked at him and came to a stop. "You look—"

He held up his hand to stop her. "Don't say it. Please. I know how I look. I feel worse, okay?"

"You earned it, Cal. You know better than that."

"I know." But even as he said it, some of the pain in his head receded. He had a feeling it had more to do with Sabrina's arrival than the miracle worked by coffee. "You brought luggage, didn't you?"

"Of course. I already put it in the other guest room." She crossed to the table and sat across from Anastasia. "'Morning," she said. "How'd you sleep?"

"Fine." The preteen didn't bother looking up from her cereal.

"I hope you checked the dump date on the milk," Sabrina said. "Your dad isn't one for keeping many groceries around. He eats out a lot, but I guess that's going to change."

Anastasia didn't respond. Cal figured the only reason he wasn't being called the bastard who wasn't her father was because of the promise of food. He supposed he should feel some small sense of victory, but he didn't. No child should understand what it was like to be hungry.

Sabrina was unaffected by the silence. She tucked her short red hair behind her ears and leaned forward. "You look much better than you did yesterday. Did you sleep well?"

"I guess."

"The clothes seem to be okay. They're a little big, but when you gain a couple of pounds, they should fit. We'll stop by the mall, too, later today to fill out your wardrobe."

"Whatever."

Sabrina glanced at Cal. "So what's the deal? You're deducting a dime from her allowance for every word she speaks?"

"No, but I did ask her to stop swearing."

Sabrina's blue eyes twinkled, although her expression stayed serious. "Maybe she doesn't know any other words. It could have been the school system."

Anastasia rolled her eyes. "I know plenty of words. I just don't want to talk to you. Why is that a big deal?"

"Oh, it's not, I guess," Sabrina said. "I understand why you want to be sullen. After all, you've got a nice place to live, a father who wants to take care of you, a fun, witty and incredibly intelligent woman who would like to be your friend, new clothes and a chance for a new life. What a drag. I'd have a long face, too."

Twelve-year-old lips twisted. "Very funny."

"See? Witty as promised." She got up and crossed to the cupboard, where she removed a bowl. When she returned to the table, she poured herself some cereal and picked up the milk.

As Cal watched her movements, he tried to figure out what was different. There was something about Sabrina this morning, something that—

He arched his eyebrows, then regretted the movement as more pain shot through his head. The woman was dressed in jeans. He'd seen her in slacks plenty of times, those loose-fitting tailored ones that always looked so businesslike. But this time she wore butt-hugging, curve-tracing, washed-enough-times-to-be-soft-as-a-baby's-rear jeans.

Hot damn! He eyed the exposed flare of her hips, the dip of her waist, before moving to her legs. Now, if he could just get her to exchange that baggy green T-shirt for something a little more form-fitting, he would be a happy man.

Anastasia finished her breakfast and stood up.

"What do you want from me?" she demanded. "I didn't ask to be here."

"I know," Sabrina said. "But you are and it's not a bad idea to make the best of things. As for what we want, I can't speak for your dad, but I'd like you to give this place a try. I doubt it can be much worse than what you've been through. You might think about being civil. Cooperating is much nicer than fighting all the time. Try a smile."

Anastasia curled her fingers up into fists. "I don't feel like smiling."

"I know, honey. It's hard to lose your family, then come to a strange place. No one is asking you to—"

Tears filled the girl's eyes. "You don't know. You don't know anything. It's horrible. It's the most horrible thing ever."

With that, she ran from the room. A few seconds later, her bedroom door slammed shut. The sound reverberated through the condo. Cal winced.

He took another sip of coffee. This was harder than he'd thought. "How long is she going to keep doing that?" he asked. "Running away and slamming doors."

Sabrina shook her head. "For as long as it works."

Seven

Sabrina pushed the grocery cart around the corner and glanced at the boxes of cereal. Why did there have to be so many choices? She looked around for Anastasia to ask the preteen what she liked best, then wondered if Cal had a preference.

She glanced at her boss who had gotten quiet in the past hour or so. "All the shopping getting to you?" she asked.

Cal shrugged. "It's not so bad." He turned, as if checking for his daughter, then lowered his voice. "She hasn't been fun, but she's been more pleasant than I expected."

Sabrina thought about Anastasia's sullen expression and lack of communication. "Gee, you weren't expecting much then, were you?"

"Not really."

Sabrina drew in a breath. "That's probably wise. I'm sure she didn't sleep that well, what with being in a strange place. This is unfamiliar for all of us and it's going to take some time to adjust."

"Yeah." Cal stared at the row of cereal and reached for a box of chocolate flavored crisps. "I haven't had these since I was a kid. I didn't know they still made them. Great." He tossed the box in the cart, then caught Sabrina's eye. "What?"

"This is your way of setting a nutritional example for your daughter?"

"They've been fortified with several essential vitamins and minerals."

"Oh, there's a defense. And when combined with milk, they're part of a wholesome breakfast."

He grinned. "Exactly. You saw the commercial, too."

"Yes. The difference is I didn't buy into it. Cal, you cannot have this kind of cereal in the house. It's disgusting."

"So is that bird feed you eat. Real people don't dine on raw grains."

"Real people can do what they want."

"Maybe but this is my house and I'm the one paying for the food."

They stared at each other. She knew she wasn't going to win this one. Cal would buy his disgusting cereal and there wasn't anything she could do about it, except maybe pick out something slightly more nutritional and hope that Anastasia had a little common sense.

"Fine." She grabbed a box of whole grain cereal and tossed it in the cart as well. "You're determined to always get your way."

"I know. It's why you like me."

She didn't reply to that. What was the point? She couldn't deny that she did like him, for an assortment of reasons. Having won the current skirmish, he strolled ahead of her. She watched him go, trying not to notice the way he moved with an easy male grace. His legs were long and muscled. His butt, well, religions had been based on less impressive shrines. He was a package worth remembering, but not for her. She might be susceptible, but she wasn't stupid.

She followed him up the aisle. "You're going to have to hire a housekeeper," she said. "Now that Anastasia is living with you, cleaning people every couple of weeks aren't going to be enough. Someone will have to cook and be there to look after her when she comes home from school. Maybe a live-in, or at least someone full-time."

"I agree."

"I'll add it to my list of things to do," she said, having known when she mentioned the subject that she would be the person calling the agencies and interview candidates. It was, after all, part of her job. "Until we get someone in, I can take care of the cooking."

Cal looked surprised. "You can cook?"

"Most people can fix a few things. Don't look so surprised. I make a terrific spaghetti sauce, not to mention a meatloaf that could win awards."

"A woman of many talents. What else have you been keeping from me?"

Brown eyes focused on her. She felt her heart pick up the pace a little. Ignore this, she reminded herself. Cal was her boss and nothing else.

"You'll have to wait and find out," she told him, then deliberately turned away to study the display of coffee. Perhaps reading about different kinds of beans would be enough to distract her.

Anastasia rounded the end of the aisle and started toward them. She was still too thin, but at least she looked better in her new clothes. She was pale, but she would tan quickly, Sabrina thought, then added sunscreen to the lengthy shopping list.

"I forgot to ask," Sabrina said as the girl got closer. "Do you have any food allergies?"

The preteen shrugged. "I hate vegetables."

Sabrina shot Cal a warning glance before he chimed in that he did, too. "Hating isn't the same as being allergic, so the short answer is no, right?"

Anastasia's mouth twisted into a frown. "Vegetables make me throw up."

"Oh, is that all? You're going to have to work harder than that if you plan to avoid eating them." She made a couple of notes on her list.

Anastasia tossed a box of cupcakes into the cart. Sabrina stared at the treat. She'd forgotten what it had been like when she'd shopped with her brother and sisters, but it was all coming back.

"I'm buying enough food for about six days," Sabrina said. "You're welcome to select a treat for yourself, but only one and it has to last all six days. So if you want that box of cupcakes, it's fine with me. But that's it. No chips, no candy. Or you take it back and pick something else. It's up to you."

Anastasia stared at her uncomprehending. "He's rich."

Sabrina assumed the "he" in question was Cal, and that the statement about him being rich meant that money wasn't an issue.

"So?" she asked.

"So I should get what I want."

"That would be a no. There aren't many 'shoulds' in this household. However, there are plenty of 'wills' as in you will follow the rules and this is one of them. You can get what we decide you can get, and for now, that means one treat for the week. I would suggest picking something with six servings so you can enjoy it every day, but that's up to you."

Sometime during the conversation Cal had come up behind her. Sabrina felt his presence. For a second she wondered if he was going to contradict her, but he didn't. When Anastasia turned her attention to him, he grinned. "She's right, kid."

The girl grabbed the box of cupcakes. "I hate you both," she said, and started down the aisle.

"That was pleasant," Sabrina said, trying to keep her voice even. She had known it was going to be tough; she'd even known she was going to be more involved with Anastasia than her job description indicated. But being right wasn't always enough to make up for the difficulties of the moment.

"I know what you're thinking," Cal said.

"Somehow I doubt that."

"You're thinking that she's scared and alone and that she needs to figure out how far she can push us."

Sabrina stared at him in surprise. "I would have guessed the 'alone and scared' part, but I hadn't thought about boundary testing. You're exactly right. This is an unfamiliar situation for her, and she needs to learn how far she's allowed to go at any given time. I'm impressed."

"Hey, I'm an impressive kind of guy."

He was, she thought with resignation. Always had been, always would be. The truth was, Cal never lacked for female companionship because most women found him completely irresistible. No doubt Anastasia would soon join the fan club.

They rounded the next aisle and saw Anastasia reading a teen magazine. When she glanced up and noticed them, she scowled and moved away.

"She wasn't kidding," he said unhappily. "She really hates us."

"Everyone needs to adjust, Cal. You can't take it too personally."

"She's my daughter. How am I supposed to take it?"

"Slowly. Carefully. There aren't going to be any easy answers."

He nodded. "I didn't think it would be like this."

"I know." He thought it would be simple. But few things in life ever were. "The good news is, you won't have to do this on your own for very long."

"I don't have to do this on my own now. I have you."

She grabbed a couple of cans of tomatoes, along with some tomato sauce. If she was going to make Gram's famous spaghetti sauce, she needed all the ingredients. "That's not what I meant," she told him. "I'm talking about something permanent."

"You're permanent. Aren't you?"

Oops! She hadn't meant to hint at anything. "Okay, bad word choice," she said, recovering quickly. "What I'm trying to say is that I just work for you. Even if you're right about Tiffany running in the opposite direction to avoid being a stepmother, she's not the only single woman out there. A lot of them would be pleased to help you with Anastasia. In fact, you're going to have to be careful, because more than a few of them will use Anastasia to get to you."

"Great." He shoved his hands into his jeans pockets. "I'm not going to worry about it now. I can't imagine going out with anyone. As far as I'm concerned, the only two females in my life are you and my daughter."

She told herself that her sudden response was triggered by the sight of him walking in front of her, which gave her far too much opportunity to stare at his rear. Or maybe it was guilt over the fact that she was really going to contact those headhunters to find out if there was life after Calhoun Jefferson Langtry. Or maybe it was that she was tired from not having slept much the previous night. Whatever the reason, when Cal said she was one of the two females in his life, she wanted to melt. Right there…knees buckling, muscles giving way until she was just a puddle in the canned goods aisle.

"How long is that going to last?" she asked, then went on without waiting for an answer. "My point is, you're not always going to be on your own with Anastasia. You two will come to some kind of understanding, then you'll find someone and it will all work out."

"That's really likely. Thanks."

She ignored his sarcasm and continued down the aisle. Sabrina paused in front of the magazines and picked up the current issue of one popular with girls Anastasia's age. "For later," she said, hiding it under a package of paper towels. "Surprise her when things are going well. She'll like it."

"You're assuming that will happen before the issue is outdated," he muttered.

Sabrina chuckled. "So the surly nature is inherited. Like father, like daughter?"

"I am not surly."

"I can see that. You're also not cranky when you don't get your own way."

He gave her his steely-eyed glare. It worked on most business opponents, but she'd seen it enough to be pretty immune.

"Yup," she said. "Just like I thought. Surly. I'll bet you were a sulker, too, when you didn't get your own way as a kid."

"I resent this, Sabrina. Make no mistake, you are an employee and can be replaced."

She laughed. "Uh-huh. Sure, Mr. Langtry."

Before he could reply, Anastasia approached the cart. She had a bag of chips in one hand and chocolate in the other. "This is what I want," she said. "Both of them."

Sabrina stared at her. She knew she'd been speaking English just a few minutes ago. Then she recognized the challenge in the girl's eyes. Fine, if she wanted to do a little testing, Sabrina was more than up to the task.

Cal shifted uncomfortably. "Well, the bag of chips looks small," he said. "It wouldn't last a chipmunk for a week."

Sabrina looked at him. He clamped his lips together and nodded. "Okay. One treat, Anastasia. Just one. Decide."

His daughter glared at him, then tossed the candy into the cart. "I can't believe you're doing this," she said before she flounced off.

"Me, neither," Cal said softly, watching her go. "Jeez, Sabrina, I wouldn't be able to get through this without you. I feel like I'm going to mess up every time I turn around."

"You'll get the hang of it. I have the advantage of younger siblings that I helped raise. But it's not so hard."

"That's what I tell everyone about finding oil, but no one believes me." He touched her upper arm. "Thanks."

He headed for the front of the store. Sabrina forced herself to concentrate on her list rather than watching her boss walk away. The tingling in her arm subsided after a couple of seconds and she was soon able to draw in an undisturbed breath.

This whole situation was incredibly dangerous to

her. She hadn't seen that at first, but she was figuring it out, and fast. Normally they spent a lot of time together, but there was always business between them. Even when they traveled, it wasn't *personal*. But this was. Having to deal with Anastasia put them into a situation they'd never experienced before. They were talking about many things best left unsaid, seeing sides of each other that should remain hidden. Cal could probably get through this without giving any of it a moment's thought, but she wasn't that disinterested. No matter how she tried to ignore the reality, the man got to her.

Him needing her, depending on her, the sudden intimacy of family, all conspired to make her think about belonging…about this being real.

"You know better," she said aloud. She'd always known better. She wasn't Cal's type, he didn't find her attractive, and even if he did, what was the point? Cal thrilled to the chase, but once he'd caught his flavor of the month, he wasn't that eager to keep her around. She didn't want a brief affair. Actually she didn't know what she wanted, but she believed with all her heart it was much safer to stay professional, no matter how strong the temptation to make it more.

Cal watched as Sabrina stepped into his study and hit the switch by the door. He blinked in the sudden light.

"What are you doing?" she asked.

"Sitting in the dark," he said. "Pretty pathetic, huh?"

He leaned back in his desk chair and motioned for her to take a seat on the leather sofa by the bookcase. She did as he requested.

"Want to talk about it?" she asked.

"I'm not sure there's anything to say. I feel as if I'm in the middle of a war, but I can't figure out if I'm the enemy or she is."

The "she" in question was, of course, his daughter, he thought. Right now Anastasia was watching television in the other room. She'd spent the later afternoon and early evening alternating between vaguely pleasant and a complete brat.

"You want a drink?" Sabrina asked as she rose and moved to the wet bar in the corner.

"No, thanks. I tried that last night and all that happened was I woke up feeling lousy."

"I think I want to double-check your findings," she said, and poured herself a small glass of brandy. She carried the snifter back to the sofa and took a seat.

They sat in silence for a while. The lamplight made Sabrina's red hair glow like fire. He'd always been a man who preferred blondes, but there was something appealing about her bright coloring. With her face partially in shadow, her eyes looked more smoky gray than blue, but they were still large and fringed with dark lashes. She'd been in her jeans all day, but he hadn't gotten used to seeing the actual shape of her hips and thighs. To be honest, he liked it. Sabrina wasn't model thin. She had curves, like a real woman. Curves a man could cup and stroke and—

Down boy, he ordered himself. He had no business going there. Sabrina was off limits for a lot of reasons. For one, she was an employee, and he didn't mess around where he did his business. For another, she deserved his respect. Finally, he wasn't stupid. If he made a pass at Sabrina, she would probably haul off and hit him. Worse, she might want to quit, and right now he couldn't survive without her.

"Who would have thought it would come to this," he said.

"Meaning you never thought you would be a father?"

The question surprised him. "Maybe. Kids." He shook his head. "I suppose they were part of my plan, but a vague part, somewhere in the distant future. I never expected to have one thrust upon me like this. Anastasia and I are a real pair. God knows what she needs from me, but it's unlikely I'm going to be able to provide it."

"I think you're selling yourself short," Sabrina told him. "So far, you're doing fine."

"Yeah, right. She told me I should have known about her. I should have made it my business to know, or somehow sensed it."

"You know that's not true," Sabrina said gently. "You don't have psychic powers. She's thinking in terms of fairy tales and television. This is real life."

"Maybe she's right. Maybe I should have known."

Sabrina leaned forward. "How?"

"If you're going to get logical, we can't have this discussion," he warned.

"Oh, I see. So you should have had a dream or a vision?"

She had a point. "I understand that Anastasia is reacting from the point of view of a hurt child, but she's not completely off base with her accusations. If I didn't know about her, I should have at least had a clue about Janice. I was intimate with the woman. How could I have let her deceive me that way?"

"You didn't *let* her do anything. She tricked you.

She deliberately set out to get pregnant. You couldn't have predicted that.''

She was right. He knew that in his head, but his gut told him otherwise. In his gut, a voice whispered that there had been clues, but he'd missed them.

''Maybe you'd feel better if you pounded on the wall and called her a name,'' she suggested.

''Always practical.''

''Just trying to help.''

''Thanks, but I don't think breaking my hand is going to improve my mood. Besides, Janice isn't the only person I blame for this mess.''

''The other two are your parents, aren't they?''

He nodded. His parents. The two people who were supposed to love him and look out for him. Instead, they'd made decisions for him, had kept the truth from him.

''They had no right,'' he said, trying to block the tide of anger swelling inside him. ''I know they were reacting to years of dealing with Tracey. I can't remember how many times she ran away, how many times she thought she was pregnant. It was grim for everyone.''

''It's going to take some time to come to terms with this,'' Sabrina said.

Cal wasn't sure he ever would. ''They never gave me the chance to make a choice.''

''Because they knew what you would do. Maybe you're looking at this all wrong. There is a bright side.''

He raised his eyebrows. ''Illuminate me.''

''The big concern for your folks was that once you found out about Janice, you would want to marry her, or at the very least, take responsibility for the child.''

"So?"

"So?" She smiled. "Cal, what does that say about the kind of person you are? They knew you would do the right thing. Even then, they knew you were a good man whom they couldn't manipulate. That speaks highly of your character. That should make you happy."

He didn't think he could use that word to describe his state of mind right now, but he understood her point. "You know the real tragedy in this?" he asked. "My mother won't want anything to do with her. Anastasia is her only grandchild. But my mother will never forget who Janice wasn't, in terms of money and social standing. So she won't bother. I can forgive a lot, but I know I'll never forgive her that."

"That's good," Sabrina said. "You seem to have all the characteristics of a great father in the making. Maybe we should get a couple of books on parenting to bring you up to speed. After all, your daughter is practically a teenager."

He groaned. "I don't want to think about that."

"It's going to happen whether you want it to or not. It won't be so bad. At least funding her college tuition isn't going to be a hardship."

As consolations went, it wasn't much of one. What Sabrina didn't understand and what he couldn't find it in himself to explain was that he was terrified. How was he supposed to father this soon-to-be young woman who had entered his life? He'd never been very good at relationships of any kind, let alone important ones. He had a few friends from his school days that he was still in touch with, but only on a casual basis. He'd been involved with women, but never for very long. Hell, if the truth be told, Sabrina was not only his most reliable friend, but his most successful relationship, and they got along because they'd never tried to make it personal. He didn't know how to love someone, and he knew instinctively that's what his daughter needed most.

"College," he said. "That's so far off. It's late May and I'm worried about getting through the summer. School doesn't start until August. What are we going to do until then?"

"We'll figure something out," she promised.

He knew she was right. Somehow they would struggle through this. "So I should probably put some money in a mutual fund for her," he said. "For her education."

"Not a bad idea."

He looked at her. "Did you get your college loans paid off? I know you had a scholarship and a grant, but didn't you owe money?"

She laughed. "Oh, Cal, I took care of that years ago. I believe it was my bonus the second year that paid off those debts. And before you ask, I've already taken care of my siblings' college and Gram. There's plenty of money."

He nodded. He was glad she was okay. Now she could put something aside for herself. Knowing Sabrina, she already had. "So you're saying you don't have to work for a living?"

"I do have to work, but not very hard."

He'd been teasing when he'd asked his question and she'd responded in kind. But instead of chuckling with her, he was struck with an unwelcome thought. That she didn't need him anymore.

Her job was interesting, he knew that. She enjoyed the travel, the different people she met, but she didn't *have* to work for him. Not like at the beginning, when her family had depended on her.

So why did she stay?

The question startled him, and he didn't want to think of an answer. What if there wasn't one? What if he couldn't come up with a good reason for Sabrina to stay? How long would it be before she figured out she would be better off somewhere else?

As he had the night before, he wandered the halls. It was after midnight and he couldn't sleep. This time Cal couldn't blame the alcohol, mostly because he hadn't had any to drink. Worries, concerns, what if's, all conspired to keep him awake.

He walked toward the two guest rooms. Both doors were closed. He paused outside of Sabrina's but didn't open it. He wondered if she was awake and what she wore to bed. A sensible pair of pajamas, or maybe an oversize cotton T-shirt? Or did she wear something sexy and soft, keeping that side of her nature private?

Error, he thought as his mental questions formed images that had his blood heading south. That was inappropriate and dangerous. So he left his assistant's door and moved to his daughter's.

Here he did turn the knob and peek inside. As she had the night before, Anastasia lay on her side facing him. She clutched the teddy bear close to her chest, hugging it as if she would never let go. By day the toy was tossed casually in a corner as if she didn't want anyone to know how much it mattered, but at night it was her talisman against the scary place that was her world.

He ached for her. In his heart he felt a distinct thaw of emotions, and he sent up a prayer that God would

help him to figure out how on earth he was going to
be anything close to a decent father.

His gaze settled on her, on her pretty features, her
thin shape under the covers. She appeared more vulnerable in the dead of night, more at risk, and he
wanted to protect her. The problem was, he didn't have
a clue as to how.

Eight

When Cal walked into the kitchen he noticed two things. One was the smell of coffee, the other was the sight of Sabrina standing with her back to him. The coffee would get his blood flowing, something he needed after a second restless night. And Sabrina, well, she was part of his world and he liked that she was there when he woke up.

She turned toward him and held out a steaming mug. "'Morning, boss," she said.

She was fresh from the shower. Her hair was still a little damp, her face scrubbed clean. She didn't wear a lot of makeup, but he rarely saw her without any. Her skin was faintly freckled, her lashes a little on the pale side. She looked wholesome, he decided. Like a young woman selling dairy products in a television commercial.

He let his gaze linger over the blue T-shirt she'd tucked into white shorts. Her feet were bare, and he was surprised to see that she painted her toenails a soft peach. Interesting.

He sipped the coffee and moved to the table. His daughter was already sitting there. She looked at him, dark eyes staring, measuring. He braced himself for the opening salvo. Anastasia didn't let him down.

"What are you going to do with me?" she asked abruptly. "You can't take me shopping every day.

School's out, so you won't be able to dump me there, at least not for a while. Plus you have a job, right? I mean you have to do something, you're not just rich.''

Cal didn't know how to answer the question of what to do with her, nor did he feel he had to justify his existence or his employment. Still, her comments were valid. What *was* he going to do with her? Unfortunately, he hadn't had enough coffee to get his brain going.

Sabrina crossed to the table and put her hand on the girl's shoulders. ''That's not a very pleasant way for anyone to start their day, is it? What about saying 'good morning,' or even just 'hi'?''

Anastasia blushed and ducked her head. ''Hi,'' she mumbled, then shoved a big spoonful of cereal into her mouth.

''Good morning,'' he said, and took the seat opposite her. ''Did you sleep well?''

She nodded.

A pleasant almost-conversation. It wasn't much, but it was progress. He glanced at Sabrina. She grinned. He returned the smile and something flashed between them.

Cal was so startled that, had he been drinking, his coffee would have gone down the wrong way. He couldn't define the flash, but in its aftereffect, he found himself wanting to walk around the table, pull her close and kiss her.

The thought was more unexpected than unpleasant. Kiss Sabrina? Where had that come from? It's not that she wasn't attractive, in her own way, she just wasn't his type. In his mind, she'd always been more office equipment than actual female.

Strange, he thought. Maybe it was the change in circumstances, or the shorts. He eyed her long legs. They were shapely enough. If she were a different kind of woman or he was a different kind of man, he would enjoy imagining them wrapped around his waist, pulling him closer as he—

Enough, he ordered himself. This was too dangerous. He needed Sabrina, and he wasn't about to risk messing everything up now. Not when he had a new daughter to worry about. Sabrina was his lifeline with Anastasia.

He smiled slightly as he took another drink of coffee. If the truth were told, even if he wanted to start something, he wouldn't have a chance with Sabrina. She knew him too well, knew his patterns with women. If she thought he was the least bit interested, she would run screaming in the opposite direction. She often told him he was a complete cad—even though she agreed he didn't do it on purpose.

"How about a bagel," Sabrina said, moving back to the counter.

"Sounds great."

She sliced one and popped it into the toaster, then carried over a bowl of fresh fruit.

She moved around his kitchen with a familiarity he lacked, even though it was his place, not hers. He didn't do much cooking, preferring to eat out with friends, or Sabrina, if he didn't have a date. She was, he realized with some small shock, his best friend. When had that happened?

Before he could find an answer or even decide how he felt about the revelation, Sabrina handed him a plate with his bagel and a container of cream cheese. She took the seat next to his and served herself a bowl of fruit.

"Anastasia has a point," she said. "We are going to have to find some things for her to do. I suspect it's too late for summer camp, but I can check."

Anastasia rolled her eyes. "Camp? I'm not a kid."

"You're twelve," Sabrina pointed out. "You're not an adult yet, therefore, by definition, you *are* still a kid. Some camps are fun."

"How would you know? Have you ever been to one?"

"Nope. I grew up poor." Sabrina made the statement cheerfully. "But then I had a brother and two sisters to keep me company, not to mention a warm and friendly personality that allowed me to have lots of friends."

Anastasia opened her mouth, then clamped it shut.

A second bagel popped out of the toaster. Sabrina retrieved it and continued her conversation. "But we are going to have to come up with some kind of a plan. Not just for the summer, but also for the fall. Where is she going to school?"

Cal finished with the cream cheese and passed it to her. "Isn't there one close by? She'll be in middle school, right?" He looked at his daughter. "Sixth grade."

"Yes."

"Middle school is a possibility," Sabrina said slowly. "But there's an excellent all-girls' school not too far from here. I've heard wonderful things about it. They do a great job with manners and social skills, as well as academic subjects."

Anastasia's face paled as her eyes widened with horror. "A girls' school?" She turned to him. "You wouldn't do that to me, would you?"

He caught Sabrina's wink and had to smother a

smile. "I haven't made a decision yet. Let's see how the next few weeks go."

Anastasia looked as if she was going to protest, but she seemed to decide it wasn't the right time. She nodded once, then pushed back her chair. "May I please be excused?" she asked tightly.

Cal waved her off. "Of course."

She nearly ran from the room.

Sabrina took a bite of her bagel and chewed. Her expression was completely smug.

"You did that on purpose," he accused.

She shrugged. "She has good manners and can be pleasant when she wants to be. But most of the time, she's a little witch. I understand that adjusting is going to take time, but I don't want her thinking she has the upper hand. One of my sisters went through a stage like this. It was hideous. Gram kept saying all she needed was firm rules, consistent discipline and plenty of love. I'm hoping it will work with Anastasia as well as it did with Melissa."

Cal understood about firm rules and being consistent, but he wasn't sure about the love part. Growing up, he always felt his parents were only interested in him for bragging rights. As long as he did what they expected and didn't embarrass them in front of their friends, they were content to leave him and his sister in the care of the ever-changing staff. Tracey had fought against the neglect by rebelling. He'd made his own life, one that didn't include family. He'd made it a point to never care too much about anyone, and that philosophy had eventually become second nature. He wasn't sure he could go back and learn to love, even if he wanted to.

Sabrina finished her bagel and took the plate to the sink. "Let me get my notes," she said. "There are a few pressing issues." She grinned. "Some of them are even about work."

While she collected her papers and her computer, he poured them each more coffee and settled back in his chair.

"Ada says they hit oil, just like you expected," Sabrina said, handing him a lengthy fax.

Over the next half hour, they got through the faxes and notes. Cal put down the last paper. "How are the interviews going to replace old octopus hands?"

She consulted a file in her laptop. "According to the memo Ada sent me, it's down to three people, all women, all highly qualified. Someone will be in place by the middle of next week."

"Good."

Sabrina hit a couple of keys. "All right, now that the easy stuff is taken care of..."

Her voice trailed off and he groaned. "I know. Anastasia. I know she wasn't polite about it, but you and she did have a point this morning. We are going to have to do something with her. It's only late May. From what I remember, school doesn't start until mid-August. As she said, we can't spend every day at the mall."

"If I were an incredibly cruel person, I would tell you this is not part of my job description and that you're on your own with this one," Sabrina teased. "But I'm not."

He ignored her threat, mostly because he knew it was meaningless. Sabrina would never leave him in a lurch.

"What about summer camps?" he asked. "*Is* it too late?"

"It is for the one at Rice University. It's been full

for months." Sabrina rested her elbow on the table and her chin on her hand. "The problem is, neither of us knows anyone with kids her age. Well, that's not completely true. Ada has a couple of nieces about her age, but we can't impose on her too much. Anastasia likes to read and there are always videos, but that's a solitary way for someone to spend the summer. I'd like to see her get out and make some friends. Then she wouldn't feel so alone."

"It might improve her disposition, too," he grumbled. He consoled himself with the fact that it was going to get better, and at least her comebacks showed that she was a fast thinker and incredibly bright.

"I could check the local parks program," Sabrina said, typing on her keyboard. "Maybe there's an art school or something."

She focused on the computer. Cal watched as her gaze narrowed. She sat cross-legged in the kitchen chair, which she rarely did at the office. Her hair had dried and fluffed up some, with a couple of wisps brushing against her cheek.

He raised his hand toward her face, as if to tuck the curls behind her ear, then pulled back. The gesture was too personal, which was odd, because he'd hugged her before and hadn't thought twice about it.

She wrinkled her nose. "Swimming, maybe? Lessons if she doesn't know how. It's too hot for tennis. Some kind of club." She pressed more keys.

How long had she been pretty, he wondered. He remembered when she'd first hired on. He'd thought she was presentable, but nothing even close to his type. At the time, that had been a blessing. The last thing he'd wanted was to be attracted to his personal assistant. But she was pretty now. Had she changed or had he? Was it just the circumstances, their being thrown together in a way that hadn't happened before?

Pretty was all right, he told himself. She could be pretty, and he could even think about wanting her. Sex was completely safe. It was the liking that got him into trouble, and that was part of the problem. While he'd just figured out that Sabrina was pretty, he'd always liked her. So what the hell was he going to do about that now?

"I think she's darling," Ada said three days later, then took a sip of her coffee. "So sweet and well mannered. Do you know she actually came into the kitchen and asked if she could help me with dinner last night? You tell Cal he got lucky with that young lady. My nieces are great and I love them, but they have no manners at all."

They were sitting in Sabrina's office, on the sofa that faced the window. Sabrina set her cup on the glass coffee table and stared at her secretary.

"We *are* talking about the same girl, right? About five six, dark hair and eyes, glasses, Cal's new daughter?"

Ada dismissed her with a wave. "Don't you dare say anything bad about her. She's a charmer. I adore her. She can come and stay with me anytime. I don't care if my nieces are spending the night with me or not. I'd love to take her out and spoil her with shopping and movies." The older woman smiled. "You just want to hug her."

Sabrina's phone buzzed. "You around?" Cal asked.

She stood up and crossed to her desk. "Right here. Want me to come up?"

"Please."

"Be right there." She released the button. "Sorry, Ada, the boss calls."

"No problem." Her secretary started for the door. "Tell Cal what I said. I'm happy to baby-sit or whatever. Anastasia is a wonderful girl."

Sabrina was still shaking her head when she walked into Cal's office.

"I'm brilliant," he said, handing her a file.

She glanced at the tab and raised her eyebrows. "This is about the joint venture. Did you get a meeting finalized?"

He grinned. "For next month, in Hong Kong. If you're very good, I'll let you come and we can go back to your favorite Chinese restaurant."

"The one we ate at last year when I won our stock bet?" she asked.

He glared at her. "That would be the one, yes. Put it on the calendar."

"Okay." She made a note in the file. "I was just talking to Ada about Anastasia's visit."

Cal leaned back in his chair and loosened his tie. It was late in the afternoon, and he'd long since rolled up his shirtsleeves to the elbows. Now he opened his collar and tossed his tie onto the desk.

"How bad was she?" he asked.

"According to Ada, your daughter is sweet, well mannered and a charmer."

Cal stared at her. "This is my daughter we're talking about? Anastasia? The same one who called me a sperm donor?"

"That would be her. Apparently she knows how to be polite, she simply chooses not to be around us."

"Great. I feel so special."

Sabrina leaned toward him. "Cal, you know she's

testing you. She's still scared about being here and not sure you're going to keep her."

"I don't mind the testing," he grumbled, "but I'm ready to get a grade already. If I had to pick, I suppose it's better that she's well behaved outside the home."

Sabrina laughed. "Oh, Lord, you're turning into a parent. Have you been reading those child-rearing books I gave you?"

"I've skimmed a couple. I don't think I agree with everything they say, but it's interesting." His warm gaze settled on her. "Thanks for all your help, Sabrina. I couldn't have gotten through the last week without you."

"No problem. It's kinda fun. After all, if she gets really hideous, I can escape back to my own place." She made the statements lightly, but inside she felt the heavy weight of guilt.

While she was happy to help Cal, she knew she wasn't going to be around as long as he thought she was. So far she'd spoken to a couple of different head-hunters, and both of them had felt she wouldn't have any trouble finding work with another company. Between her education and her unique work experience, she was a prize. Sabrina didn't feel very prizelike at the moment, but maybe a job offer or two would change that.

She pushed the guilt aside and reminded herself that she wasn't doing anything wrong. She'd been a good and loyal employee for Cal, but she hadn't signed a lifetime contract. She needed to make her own way in the world, and that wasn't going to happen while she was with him.

His phone rang and he picked up the receiver. She watched him, the way the afternoon sun brought out the gold highlights in his brown hair. He was so hand-some—it wasn't fair. How was she supposed to resist his good looks along with everything else? Life would be a whole lot easier if she could just hate her boss. But she didn't. She liked him…a lot. They were friends and she knew she would miss him when she left.

When he hung up, she glanced at her watch. "I've got to go pick up Anastasia. The movie gets out in twenty minutes and there's going to be traffic." She rose to her feet and crossed to the door. "Don't use this as an excuse to work late, young man. I'm not your live-in baby-sitter."

"Yes, ma'am. I have a couple calls to make, then I'll come straight home." His grin broadened. "What's for dinner, dear?"

"I'm thinking of a couple of words," she called over her shoulder as she headed for the door. "They're not polite words. Actually, the second one is fine. It's the first one that's gonna get me in trouble."

She was still chuckling over their conversation when she pulled up in front of the movie complex. Anastasia was waiting with two other preteens. They all saw her, and Ada's nieces waved. Anastasia said something to them, then walked to the car.

"Hi," Sabrina said when she climbed in and fastened her seat belt. "How was the movie?"

"Okay, I guess."

"Ada said you had fun last night."

Anastasia looked out the window. "Uh-huh."

"She also ratted you out, kid. So the act isn't going to fly for much longer."

Anastasia stared at her. "What do you mean she ratted me out? I didn't do anything wrong. I was polite and everything."

"I know. That's my point. She told me you were a pleasure to be around, well mannered and all the rest. So how come you give us the surly treatment at home?"

Instead of the flip comeback she'd expected, Anastasia turned back to the window and sniffed. "I d-don't know."

"Yes, you do. We all do. I understand that you're scared, but it's going to be fine. You have to trust that."

"Who are you?" Anastasia asked. "You work for my dad, but now you're living at his place. But you're not the housekeeper. It's too weird. I don't know you and I don't know him. I miss my parents. I just want things back the way they were before."

"I know, honey. It's hard."

A strangled sob caught in her throat. "You don't know."

Sabrina sighed. "Actually, I do. I was fourteen when my parents were both killed in a car accident. It was the most horrible experience of my life."

Anastasia looked at her. "Yeah?"

Sabrina nodded. "I would have given anything to have them back. I couldn't figure out what I'd done wrong to make them go away. I mean, I knew it was an accident, but I didn't believe it."

The preteen wiped at her tears. "I know," she whispered.

"I had my brother and two sisters to help me get through it. I also had a grandmother, but it was still awful. You've had a difficult year, but now you have a father who very much wants to be a part of your life. He care about you."

"He doesn't even know me. How can he care?"

Then Sabrina got it. She wondered why she hadn't seen it before. While Anastasia was fighting the fear of an unfamiliar place and different circumstances, she was also terrified that her new father wouldn't like her. After all she'd been through, she wouldn't survive another rejection in her young life. It was safer to lash out, to create distance so nothing could hurt her ever again.

"You're not making it easy for him, are you?" she asked softly.

"Why should I?"

Good point, Sabrina thought. That was the parent's job, not the child's.

"He's just playing at being a father. He's not interested in me at all."

Sabrina heard a familiar echo in those words. "That's not you talking," she said. "That's your aunt."

Shrug. "Does it matter? It's the truth."

"No, it's not, but I guess you're going to have to wait and see who's right on that one."

They were silent for the rest of the drive. Something was going to have to be done, Sabrina thought. Cal and his daughter needed a chance to bond, and it wasn't going to happen under the present circumstances. Cal needed to spend time with the girl, but in such a way that it wasn't forced or too awkward for either of them. And she knew just how to make that happen.

"This is getting to be a habit," Cal said as Sabrina joined him in his study. It was nearly ten and Anastasia was in bed.

Sabrina smiled. "A nice one, I hope." She poured

them each a brandy and sat in the chair across from his desk.

"Very nice." He took a sip of the drink. It *was* nice. He enjoyed having her in his house. He liked the close contact, finding her in the kitchen first thing in the morning, the way she insisted on taking her own car to the office because she would need it to pick up Anastasia. He liked talking with her about his concerns, listening to her opinion—she had one on everything—watching her absently touch his daughter's hair or shoulder in an unconscious gesture of affection.

Nights were the best...and the worst. He couldn't stop thinking about her at night. He looked forward to the moment she would walk into the study and take a seat. He liked looking at her in the subtle light. He enjoyed watching her relax, kick off her shoes and slump down in the chair. Sometimes, if he wasn't careful, his mind took the image further. To her slowly peeling off her blouse and letting it fall to the floor, followed by her bra. He pictured her bare breasts, the peach-colored tips pouting at him as they puckered. He thought about himself circling the desk and pulling her close, kissing her, holding her, running his hands all over her back and shoulders before finally—

"A penny for your thoughts," she said. "You're a million miles away."

He shifted uncomfortably as he realized he was rock hard. Thank God the desk was between them. "Not that far," he told her. "And definitely not worth a penny."

"If you say so." She slumped down in her chair. "I had an interesting talk with Anastasia when I picked her up from the movies. Apparently her aunt said that you were just playing at being a father and Anastasia is afraid that's true. She's not willing to give you the benefit of the doubt because she can't afford to be wrong. If she starts to care about you, then loses you, she won't be able to recover. The girl has no emotional reserves.''

Cal listened to the words and shook his head. ''Great. It makes sense, but how do I change that? She's barely civil to me, let alone pleasant. I don't know what to say to her or what to do with her.'' He ran his hand through his hair. There was nothing like a little emotional inadequacy to take care of a man's libido. The last lingering physical traces of desire faded.

Anastasia was smart to be wary of him. He didn't know the first thing about parenting and he was bound to screw it all up. ''Maybe I should have made other arrangements for her,'' he muttered. ''Sent her to people who know what they're doing.''

''Don't even think that,'' Sabrina told him. ''You're her father and you want to care about her. All the expertise in the world can't take the place of that. Give it time, Cal. It's barely been a week. You two will figure out how to be a family. I've been thinking about this, and one of the problems is location.''

He glanced around the study. ''You don't like my condo?''

''No. It's fine. The problem is that it's summer break, she doesn't have any friends or ways to fill her time. You've got work, I have my own life. So no one is a hundred percent focused on the problem. I suggest a vacation. The three of us go away, maybe for a month or so, and you two spend some time getting to know each other.''

As long as Sabrina was going to be there to keep

him from making too big a mistake, he was in favor of the idea. "Where would you like to go?"

"Maybe the beach."

"Corpus Christi is a great idea. I know a couple—"

Sabrina covered her face with her hands and groaned. "Not there, Cal. It's still the gulf and really hot. Let's go somewhere nice and cool. I was thinking of Balboa Island in Southern California. It's a little crowded, but fun. There's lots to do and it's not like a steam bath."

He chuckled. "You still haven't adjusted to the Texas summers, have you?"

"No, and I don't want to adjust. Come on. A month on the California shore. Balboa would be fun. There's boating and the beach. We could go in-line skating. Disneyland is about thirty minutes away. Some of the restaurants in Newport are fabulous, and there is the most amazing mall."

"Oh, well, a mall. You've convinced me."

She smiled at him. "Is that a yes?"

He could deny her nothing, he realized with some amazement. At that moment, he would have given his soul to make Sabrina happy. What was happening to him?

"Cal? Say yes."

"Yes," he told her, because he didn't have a choice.

Nine

The sun had set a couple of hours before, but it wasn't completely dark down by the beach. There were lights from other houses, the streets and the docks, not to the mention the glow from the amusement area on the peninsula.

Sabrina settled back in her chair and sighed. "This is how the good Lord intended life to be," she said. "The water, the stars, the cool night air." She glanced at her boss. "Cool air. You remember that, Cal, don't you? I realize it's been about four months since summer started in Houston, but we did have those three days of spring. It was cool then."

"I get enough sass from my daughter," he said. "I don't need to hear it from you, too."

"Sure you do. It keeps you in touch with the little people."

His response was a grunt, a surefire signal he wanted the subject changed. Sabrina chuckled. At this point, she was so happy to be back in California and on the beach, she would have agreed to almost anything.

They sat in silence for a while. Faint music drifted to them from one of their neighbors. There was the sound of laughter and conversation.

"They must be having a party," Cal said, motioning to his left.

"Probably. Maybe next time they'll invite us."

Cal stretched out his long legs and reached for his can of soda on the plastic table beside his chair. "It's not what I thought," he admitted. "But I like it."

Property was a premium on Balboa Island, and the houses pressed up against each other. They were mostly long, narrow structures, two stories, many with apartments in back or on the second floor. Sabrina had rented a three-bedroom single family house right on the water. Their front patio opened onto the boardwalk, with the boats and the water beyond.

Anastasia was already in bed. Sabrina found herself wishing they'd left on a light in the living room so it wasn't so cozy on the patio. She wanted to inch her chair away from her boss, or maybe jump up and go for a walk. Without warning, her muscles got all twitchy and she felt as if her skin was two sizes too small.

It was the close confines of the house, it was traveling together, it was the sea air and it was the man himself. He got to her. With his good looks and his easy smile. That damn Texas drawl. Why couldn't he be a troll, or at least have a few really annoying personal habits? In the regulated world of work she found it easy to confine herself to business, but here, like this, it was too much like a real vacation, which meant her guard kept slipping. If she didn't watch her step, she was going to do something really stupid, like notice her boss was a single guy and very appealing.

She ducked her head to hide the smile. Okay, so she'd already noticed. Noticed and admired and wanted. She bit back a curse, she who rarely swore.

If she was just lusting after his body, she wouldn't be so worried. That sort of need was usually hormonal and would pass quickly. But she liked Cal. She enjoyed being around him, and sometimes she even admired him. So she was in really big trouble. This was why she'd never wanted to move into his condo. The longer they were in close proximity, the more she was at personal risk.

"This is always what I've shied away from," he said, his voice low and quiet in the night.

Her heart gave a start and she turned to look at him. Had he been reading her mind? "W-what are you talking about?" Had she accidentally said something she shouldn't or had he guessed or had—

"Commitment to something important." He angled toward her. "I'm not talking about business, of course. I mean personally. The idea of settling down with someone, having a family. I wanted to, but I figured I could avoid it for a lot longer. Now it's found me."

"Anastasia." Of course. He was talking about his daughter. She wasn't sure whether to be disappointed or relieved.

"I like her," he said, sounding surprised. "She has a real attitude, but there's something about her. When she's not trying so hard to be difficult, she's fun."

"I know what you mean. Today was pleasant." They'd spent the afternoon on the peninsula, going on the amusement rides and window shopping.

Cal chuckled. "She would rather walk through fire than admit it, but I think she was impressed about flying first class. Last time she'd been too scared and tired to notice, but on this flight, she got into it."

"She's certainly a Langtry," Sabrina agreed.

Cal leaned toward her and tugged on a lock of hair. "I'm going to ignore that," he told her. "I know you meant it in the nicest possible way."

"Oh, of course."

His humor faded and he leaned back in his chair. "She scares me. I've been looking in on her while she sleeps, and I get this knot of fear right in the center of my chest. What if I can't do it? What if I don't know how? Wanting to have a family someday in the future isn't any kind of preparation for having a twelve-year-old thrust into my life. What if I mess her up?"

His questions came from the heart. Sabrina felt the last of her defenses slipping away. This was the Cal she couldn't resist. The playboy millionaire was fun in his own way, but the genuine man had a line directly to her heart.

"You won't because you care," she said.

"How many horrible acts have been initiated in the name of good intentions?"

"Now you're being dramatic. Despite your preference for trophy girlfriends, you're a pretty decent guy. You don't lie, cheat or steal, you are faithful to your girlfriends, for the time you keep them around. You have the makings of a quality human being. Anastasia can see that, too. She makes trouble, but she knows you're interested in her welfare. You two are already learning about each other, but it takes time for forge a relationship. It's not instant. Give yourself, and her, a break."

"Easy for you to say," he grumbled. "You have experience with this. You helped your grandmother raise your younger siblings."

"You were a kid once, too. Think back to that."

He looked up at the sky. "I'd rather not. Tracey used to tell her friends we'd been raised by wolves. Unfortunately these were human wolves. The animal kind probably would have done a better job."

Sabrina thought about what she knew of his childhood and shuddered. Being rich might be nice some-times, but all the toys in the world didn't make up for parental neglect. "You turned out all right."

"Tracey didn't. She's nearly forty and she's dating boys half her age." He raised a hand. "I know, I know, it's a double standard. I suppose I shouldn't mind or be critical. If I thought they cared about her, it would be one thing, but they're all after money. We are a poor excuse for a family. I want more for Anastasia."

"You're giving her more. You're spending time with her and getting to know her. That's important."

"And I've got you. My ace in the hole." He rose to his feet, then bent over her chair. "Thanks."

He brushed a kiss across her forehead, straightened and walked into the house. Sabrina sat immobile for several seconds as she willed her heart rate to return to normal.

Cal had just kissed her. It didn't mean anything more than a friendly moment between people who'd been through a lot together. She knew that in her head. But in her heart, and other places slightly more interesting, she didn't want to believe it. She wanted to think that it meant something. She wanted him to be feeling the same heat, the same growing desire flickering through his body.

Close proximity, a charming man whom she genu-inely liked and way too many years of celibacy. It was not a good combination. If she wasn't careful, she was going to end up doing something incredibly stupid and then where would she be?

Cal strolled through the kitchen into the living room. Anastasia lay stretched out on the floor, watching television. A series of tall, slender models paraded across runways while rock music blared.

He crouched down next to his daughter. "What are you watching?"

"It's a show about the fashion industry. You know, what's going to be hot for fall, that kind of stuff." She pushed her glasses up her nose. "You wouldn't like it."

He settled next to her on the floor. A large area rug covered the bleached hardwood. After grabbing a cushion from the sofa, he shoved it under his head and prepared to get comfortable.

"How do you know?" he asked. "I might enjoy fashion. So what is hot for fall?"

She rolled her eyes. "You like those detective shows, or the business reports. This is only on another half hour, then you can change it."

"That's okay. I want to watch this with you. We can bond."

On their trip to the grocery store, he'd picked up a couple of parenting magazines. He needed the information to get the jump start he needed to catch up on this parenting stuff. It was harder than he'd thought. One of the articles had mentioned parent-child bonding, using television as a neutral medium.

He pointed at the screen. "That dress is nice."

The garment in question was long and black, with very little top and, when the model turned, almost no back. "Well, not for you," he amended.

Anastasia rose to her feet. They'd spent most of the three days they'd been in California outdoors. Despite the sunscreen Sabrina had insisted they all wear, his daughter was getting a faint tan. She'd gained a little weight and her face had lost its pinched look.

"Why are you doing this?" she asked. "I don't want to bond with you. Watch your own stuff and leave me alone."

The sharp anger in her voice shocked him. In the past couple of days, they'd actually been getting along. What had happened to change that? "Anastasia," he said, his tone warning.

"What? What are you going to do to me?"

"Anastasia, I—" A thought distracted him. He sat up and looked at her. "Who named you? Was it Janice or your adoptive parents?"

"My *mother*," she said, emphasizing the last word. "My real mother. Not Janice."

"Was it a family name? It seems a little old-fashioned."

"You want to talk about *my* name?" she asked. "You're Calhoun Jefferson Langtry and you think my name is funny?"

He realized he'd hit a nerve. "It's not funny. I think it's very pretty, if a little unusual."

"I don't care what you think." Her hands curled into fists and her eyes filled with tears. "I don't care about you at all because you never cared about me. Why didn't you use birth control? Why didn't you check on Janice? Why did you just go off and leave her? She *died!*" Her voice rose. "She died and I was all alone and no one cared about me. You're supposed to be my father. You're supposed to care, and you didn't even bother to find out the truth. You should have come for me."

She seemed to fold in on herself. Her shoulders hunched forward and her face scrunched up.

"Anastasia."

But he was too late. She turned to the stairs and

raced up. Seconds later he heard her bedroom door slam shut.

Cal rose to his feet and stared after her. What had happened? He'd come in to join her while she watched television. Instead of sharing some quiet time together, he'd obviously hurt her terribly and sent her from the room in tears.

"You okay?"

He turned and saw Sabrina standing in the doorway. "I'm the wrong person to ask." He pointed to the ceiling. "She's the one crying."

"I don't know. You look a little shell-shocked to me."

Cal sank onto the sofa. "What the hell happened? One minute we were discussing TV shows and the next—" He shook his head. "I'm the last person in the world to be raising a kid."

"For what it's worth, I think you did the right thing."

Then why did he have a knot in his gut and a cold, ugly feeling that he was destined to hurt the child he only wanted to love? "About what?" he asked.

"You didn't tell her the truth about Janice. She told you she was on the Pill, didn't she?"

"Yeah, but that's not something I felt I should share with a twelve-year-old. Anastasia's right. I should have checked. Somehow. I should have done a lot of things differently."

The problem was, he could be as logical as he wanted. Janice had lied. That wasn't his fault. He'd tried to get in touch with her, but she hadn't wanted him to find her. He had excuses for all of his daughter's accusations, save one—that he should have known about her. He bought into that theory, too. Even now he found it hard to believe that he'd had a child and never once sensed her presence in the world. He *should* have known. If he was any kind of father, he would have known.

"You're beating yourself up for being human," Sabrina said. "For what it's worth, I think that's a waste of time. You can't change that, and you can't erase the past. Today is what's important."

"Explain that to her," he said, jerking his head toward the ceiling.

"Oh, I intend to."

Sabrina left the room. She wished there was more she could say to Cal. His obvious concern and pain touched her. She wanted to find the right words to make it all better. Unfortunately only time would allow him and Anastasia to form a relationship. That and maybe a firm dose of reality.

She walked into Anastasia's room without knocking. The girl was curled up on the bed, her back to the door. She clutched her teddy bear against her chest.

"For one kid, you sure put out a lot of water," Sabrina said lightly as she sat next to the preteen and pulled her into her arms.

Anastasia came willingly. Sabrina stroked her hair and rocked back and forth. "I know," she murmured. "I know how it feels, and before you snap at me and say that I don't, I'm going to remind you that I lost my parents, too. Remember? I know this is painful and scary. The most scary part is that you're starting to like him and you don't want to. After all, what if he changes his mind and sends you to the state home? Or what if he dies, too?"

Anastasia raised her head. Tears streaked her face.

Behind her glasses, her eyelashes were spiky and wet. She sniffed. "How'd you know?"

"It's not so hard to figure out. I worried that Gram would die, or that I'd lose one of my sisters. Most of the time I didn't really care about my brother because he was a real pain."

The joke earned her a slight smile.

Sabrina brushed away the tears. "Cal is a pretty great guy. He's never been a dad, so he's gonna make some mistakes. It wouldn't be so bad to cut him a little slack. You're the experienced one in the group. Maybe you could help him along. He's got flaws, but he's not a quitter. He's committed to you, Anastasia. He's not going to send you away."

"You don't know that."

"Of course I do. I make all his appointments and he hasn't talked to anyone about getting rid of you." Sabrina took a deep breath. "He's just as scared as you are. He has this idea that he could really mess you up. We both know that's not true, but he believes it. See, when he was growing up, his parents didn't bother with him. They were gone a lot, and they thought he and his sister were just in the way. The staff took care of them. But the staff was always changing, so there wasn't ever anyone to worry about him, or love him. He wants more for you."

"But he was rich."

"He was lonely. And you know what that feels like, right?"

Anastasia nodded. "I get scared, and then I say stuff I don't really mean."

"He knows that, but it would be nice if you could tell him yourself. Honey, he just wants to love you and take care of you. I think you two could have a wonderful relationship, but you need to meet him halfway. He'll never take the place of the father you remember, but there's still room in your life for him. It's okay to love them both. Hearts are funny that way. No matter how many people we love, there's always enough room for one more.''

Anastasia hugged her bear close. ''You think so?''

''I promise.''

That evening Cal stared at the television, but he wasn't paying attention to the show. He was straining to hear something from upstairs. It had been a couple of hours. Sabrina had come down and said to let Anastasia work it out for herself, but he wasn't sure he could take much more of this. He felt that every time he turned around, he was doing something else wrong.

He heard footsteps and looked up. Anastasia paused in the entrance to the room.

''Hi,'' she said.

''Hi, yourself. You okay?''

She nodded. ''I'm—'' She cleared her throat. ''I'm sorry about what I said before. I didn't mean it. Sometimes I just—'' She shrugged. ''You know. Say stuff. I don't even want to. It just comes out. I'm sorry.''

He crossed to her in three strides. Once he reached her side, he didn't know what to say. ''Anastasia, I—''

She stared at her feet. ''I know. It's pretty dumb, huh?''

''Not at all.'' He reached and took her hand in his. ''It makes sense. But thank you for apologizing. That takes a lot of courage.''

She raised herself up on tiptoe, pressed a kiss to his cheek, mumbled a quick ''good-night'' and raced up the stairs. Cal stood staring after her. He felt like Sally

Field at the Academy Awards all those years ago when she'd said, "You like me, you really like me."

His daughter liked him. Hot damn.

He knew he was grinning like a fool and he couldn't help it. Anastasia had made him very happy. He crossed the room and stepped out onto the porch. Sabrina stood at the railing, staring out over the water.

"Did you tell her to apologize to me?" he asked.

Sabrina turned toward him. In the half light spilling out from the living room, her red hair looked darker than usual. Shorts exposed long legs, although an oversize T-shirt kept the top half of her charms completely covered.

"Anastasia?" she asked, then continued without waiting for an answer. "Of course not. I did talk to her and explain that you were her father and willing to meet her more than halfway. It was up to her to make the rest of the journey. I'm glad she decided to make it easy."

He shifted from foot to foot. "I know this is really dumb, but she kissed me good-night. For that second I felt like her dad."

"You are her dad."

He moved next to her and looked out at the water. Lights from boats reflected in the moving surface. "I can sniff out an oil field a hundred miles away, but I don't know the first thing about raising a daughter. And I'm obviously a lousy judge of women. I still believe I should have known what Janice was doing, but I never guessed."

"This is getting redundant, Mr. Langtry. None of that is your fault. You were willing to take responsibility as soon as you found out about your daughter. That's what matters. Let the past go, Cal. Worry about today and maybe a little about tomorrow. You and Anastasia have a chance to be a family together. Don't let go of that.''

He hoped Sabrina was right. "I like her," he said. "I know she's a real brat at times, but I like her."

"If you can say that after everything she's said to you, then you're going to be a great father."

Cal bumped his shoulder against hers. Sabrina bumped him back, telling herself the action was just playful. He was thrilled that Anastasia had apologized for what she'd said. It was a big step in forming a bond. He had every reason to be happy.

She was happy for him. At least that's what she told herself. She was also on fire from standing so close to him. Had he always generated this much body heat or was she just now noticing it? And when had it gotten so warm in the evenings around here? She thought it was supposed to be cool at night.

She had to get out of here, she told herself. Before she said or did something really stupid. Her hormones were out of control, she couldn't stop thinking about Cal. If only he would dress in his suits, or even jeans. But the shorts were driving her crazy, what with the way they left his powerful legs bare. Sometimes on the beach, he wore no shirt at all and exposed his flat belly and the dark hair that taunted her. She wanted to put her hands on him and see if he was as hard as he looked.

She swallowed. Hard. Bad, bad choice of words. It made her think of other things being hard, of—

Stop it! she commanded herself.

"Thanks, Sabrina."

Before she figured out what he was going to do, he turned toward her and pulled her close. She was too stunned to resist or pull back, then suddenly she found herself pressed against him—chest to chest, thigh to thigh, his face inches from hers.

"You're the best, little lady," he said, deliberately exaggerating his drawl.

He was teasing and she was slowly melting. Well, at least he would never know how she felt, or how much she wanted him to kiss her. Pride wasn't much to keep her company, but it was going to have to be enough.

"Thank you, cowboy," she said, but her voice sounded funny. Low and husky.

Cal's expression shifted from teasing to something else. Dear God, please, he couldn't guess. That would be too humiliating for words.

"Sabrina?"

She started to pull away. Really. That was her intent. But without warning, he dropped his head slightly and pressed his mouth to hers. Then she couldn't move, she couldn't think. She could only feel… The soft, firm pressure of his lips against hers, the way his hands cradled her so gently, the heat of him, his strength, the wanting that flooded her until she thought she would drown in the sweetest way possible.

She told herself it was a "thank you" kiss, that it didn't mean anything. But the seconds ticked by and he didn't bother pulling away. If anything, he deepened the pressure, as if testing…or waiting. For her? For a reaction? For her to jerk back and slap him, or did he want something else from her? Surrender?

Involuntarily, because she sure hadn't given them permission, her hands crept up his chest to link behind his neck. She raised herself up on her toes and angled her head slightly. That was it. She didn't do a single thing about his lips pressed against hers, but apparently the other cues were enough because he began to move.

He parted his lips and brushed them back and forth against hers. The gentle caress stole the last strength from her legs and she sagged against him. Her blood raced faster as a tingle started in her toes, working its way up her body, setting tiny fires of need as it went.

She'd thought about kissing Cal. Sometimes, when it was late and her defenses were down, she allowed herself to imagine what it would be like, but all that wondering hadn't even come close to reality. The taste of him, his scent, the powerful wall of muscles supporting her—he was so much more than she could have dreamed. She wasn't even sure this was real. Maybe it was a fantasy brought on by the night.

"Sabrina."

His voice was thick with desire. A shiver of anticipation rippled through her. As if he read her mind, he opened his mouth a little more and touched the tip of his tongue to her bottom lip. If she hadn't already been leaning against him, that single stroke would have brought her to her knees.

She clung to him. Her fingers curled into his muscles as she clutched his shirt. He, too, wore shorts, and the hair on his legs tickled her skin. Her breasts swelled, her nipples grew hard, and between her thighs the ache increased as her body grew slick in anticipation of a hoped-for invasion.

His tongue swept into her mouth and she was carried away. Everywhere he touched, she melted and wanted more. So much more. It was chemistry, or maybe physics, the attraction of magnets that sealed themselves together, or maybe molecules binding into more stable compounds.

One of his hands cupped her head, as if to hold her in place. As she answered his kiss, his touches and strokes, with playful forays of her own, she knew she had no intention of pulling back. But she liked the feel of his fingers in her hair.

With his other hand, he followed the curve of hip, then moved around to squeeze her rear. The contact brought her pelvis forward. She felt his hardness, the proof that he wanted her as much as she wanted him. As she'd always wanted him. It was—

Her heart froze in her chest, her breathing stopped and she knew she was going to die. Right there on the porch on Balboa Island. Words replayed in her head. *As she'd always wanted him.* It couldn't be true. Not that. Not Cal. She knew better. He didn't really care about her, not as a woman. He didn't care about anyone romantically. She knew that. Falling for him would be incredibly stupid. She'd protected herself…hadn't she?

Cal stepped back. "Sabrina, what's wrong?"

She realized she'd stopped kissing him and had dropped her hands to her sides. She shook her head, more to clear it than to answer his question. "Nothing. I'm fine. It's just…" She touched a hand to her lips. "I'd better go upstairs now."

"Sabrina, wait. I'm sorry if I offended you. I didn't mean—"

But she was already running up the stairs and she couldn't hear him. She hurried to her room and closed the door behind her. Her heart had resumed beating in her chest, but now it was pounding so hard she thought it might explode.

As she crossed to the window to stare out at the night, she fought against the tears burning in her eyes. It had happened. She hadn't known, or she would have tried to stop it. She knew better, but in this case, that wasn't enough. Perhaps she'd been foolish to think she could escape. Close proximity and genuine affection had conspired against her. For an assortment of reasons, some which made sense and some which didn't, she'd fallen in love with Cal.

When had it happened? These past few weeks? She leaned against the window frame and closed her eyes. No, it had been longer than that. She wasn't sure how long, but at least a year. Maybe she'd always loved him.

A single tear escaped and rolled down her cheek. She brushed it away. There was nothing to be done, she told herself. She was already making plans to leave, so she would be safe. Her only concern was to keep Cal from finding out the truth. In the best-case scenario he would be momentarily interested, but it would only be in the chase. Once he caught her, he wouldn't want her. The worst-case scenario would be that he would only pity her, and she couldn't stand that.

Best of all was for him to never find out. Once she was free of him, she would find a way to get over him. Then she would be fine. It wasn't as if she was going to love him forever.

Ten

Cal rinsed the lettuce in the sink, then tossed it into a drainer. After nearly a week at their beach house, Sabrina had announced it was his turn to cook dinner. He'd tried protesting, but she'd informed him that even he could grill hamburgers on the built-in barbecue in the corner of their patio. He'd tried pouting and complaining, but she'd stood firm. They'd made a quick trip to the grocery store for supplies, including an assortment of salads from the deli. So here he stood, getting together lettuce, onions and tomatoes, along with pickles and mustard.

The kitchen opened up onto the living room. Beyond that he could see Sabrina and his daughter on the patio. They were playing a board game. Although the sliding glass door was open, their voices didn't carry to him. Still, he enjoyed watching them together.

Anastasia continued to gain weight. Her face had filled out, and her eyes didn't look so huge and lost behind her glasses. In a couple of more weeks, she would lose the gaunt appearance of an underfed child. She continued to tan. Just yesterday, he'd caught a couple of teenage boys giving her a second glance. Fortunately Sabrina had noticed his reaction and had pulled him into the car before he could walk over and tell them to leave his daughter alone. She was only twelve.

Cal washed the tomatoes. As much as he wanted to change things, he couldn't. His daughter was practically a teenager, and the trauma of her dating was only a few years away. He could already feel his hair turning gray.

The sound of laughter caught his attention. He glanced up. Sabrina and Anastasia bent toward each other. The setting sunlight glinted in their hair. His daughter was dark like him, but Sabrina's hair glowed like fire. She tossed her head and flame-colored strands danced against the back of her neck.

Without wanting to, he remembered the feel of that skin against his hand. He'd touched her there, the night he'd kissed her. He'd stroked the softness, had experienced the warmth.

He told himself not to go there, but in the past two days, he hadn't been able to think about much else. What had started out as an impulsive, maybe even friendly kiss, had turned into something very different. Before he'd done it, he'd never really thought about kissing Sabrina. She wasn't that kind of woman, at least not to him. But when she'd been so close and he'd inhaled the scent of her body, something had happened. Something he couldn't explain but that he would very much like to repeat.

Sabrina. Who would have thought she could store all that passion inside and he would never have known? Once he'd gotten the idea to kiss her, he'd thought he might enjoy it, but he hadn't expected to be blown away.

Thoughts of kissing led to other thoughts...of things like making love with her. They'd fit so well together. That had surprised him. He'd liked how she felt in his arms and the way her body had pressed up against his.

He'd enjoyed the taste of her, the need he'd felt, the explosion that had nearly flared out of control. He couldn't remember the last time a woman had made him want to lose control.

Anastasia said something and Sabrina laughed again. He smiled as he watched the familiar crinkles appear at the corners of her eyes. He'd known Sabrina for years and he'd never suspected the truth about her. In his mind, she'd been a friend, an employee, someone he could work with, respect and even like. But desire? He shook his head. She wasn't his type. No obvious beauty, no flash. Just a quietly attractive, very special woman.

He wanted her. He wanted her in his bed, naked and willing. He wanted to know if there was the same magic between them as there had been when they'd kissed. Even though he knew better. He knew what happened when he went after a woman. He wanted her until he caught her. Once he'd won the chase, he was no longer interested in the prey.

He couldn't afford that with Sabrina. She was too important to him. He didn't want to have to worry about getting rid of her or having to replace her. For one thing, she was damn good at her job. For another, he would miss her. So, for the sake of his business, their friendship and his daughter, he would keep it platonic.

Which meant no more kissing.

He sliced the tomatoes and placed them on a plate, then dried off the lettuce and tore it into hamburger-size pieces. When everything else was ready and on the table, he returned to the refrigerator and reached for the hamburger patties. Of course there were going to be regrets, he thought. He regretted that he couldn't find out if they would be as good together as he imagined.

He was halfway across the kitchen when the realization hit him. The answer was so incredibly simple he didn't know why he hadn't thought of it before. It was true that he was more interested in the ''getting'' than the ''having'' where women were concerned. But he already knew and liked Sabrina. So once he had her and lost interest, all that would change was that he wouldn't want her in his bed. He would still need and trust her as both an employee and a friend. Their relationship would return to its pre-kiss uncomplicated state and his curiosity would be satisfied. The perfect solution. All he had to do was seduce Sabrina into agreeing with his plan. Fortunately, seduction was something he was very good at.

''But I don't want to,'' Anastasia whined the next afternoon.

Sabrina told herself to stay patient, that the girl was just reacting to the unfamiliar, but her patience was being stretched thin. What she wanted to say was ''Shut up. We're doing this so you'll have a good time and enjoy life, but if you want to go sulk in your own room, fine.'' Instead, she smiled brightly.

''Anastasia, in-line skating is a lot of fun. You're going to like it. The beach is a great place to learn. When we get back to Houston, you'll be able to do it there, too, because it's practically the flattest city on the planet. I've seen tons of kids your age in-line skating all over. You'll be able to meet them and hang out.''

Anastasia looked around at the boardwalk. They were outside a rental shop. It was midweek, so the skate-bike-people traffic wasn't too bad. "I'm not good at this kind of stuff. I'm gonna fall."

Cal plopped down on the bench next to his daughter. "Hey, kid, there's plenty of padding. You might end up with a bruise or two, but it'll still be fun." He leaned close and wrapped his arm around her shoulders. "Look at it this way. Sabrina and I are way older than you and we can both blade. You're young and athletic. Once you've picked up the sport, you'll be skating circles around us. Isn't that worth a couple hours of looking awkward and silly?"

The girl shrugged. "I guess."

"I guess," Cal mocked. "There's enthusiasm. I don't know, Sabrina. What do you think? Should we just lock her in the car while we go have a good time without her?"

Sabrina pretended to consider the suggestion, then shook her head. "No, let's give her a chance."

Hearing Cal teasing his daughter and watching him smile was enough to blow away her ill-temper. It wasn't Anastasia's fault, she reminded herself. She, Sabrina, had been out of sorts ever since the kiss.

She followed father and daughter into the rental shop. Telling herself it had just been a kiss didn't seem to be helping. No matter how many times she thought she'd put it into perspective, it just kept coming back. At night, before she fell asleep, she relived the moment. At odd times during the day, when Cal smiled at her, or accidently touched her, she thought about it again. To make matters worse, he seemed to be touching her a lot. It was starting to drive her crazy. Because when she thought about the kiss for very long, it was too easy to think about other things, like touching him back all over—and having him kiss her on places other than her lips.

They rented skates for the three of them, then went outside. Cal helped Anastasia into her gear while Sabrina slipped on hers. She hadn't been skating in a while, and the narrow wheels felt awkward. But after a couple of minutes, she was able to glide up and down the boardwalk.

"See," Cal said, pointing. "She's kinda old and she can do it."

Anastasia giggled. Sabrina gave him a mock glare. "'Kinda old'? I don't think so. Anyway, if I'm kinda old, what does that make you? A fossil?"

"I'm a man in my prime. Everyone knows women don't age as well."

"Hit him!" Sabrina commanded. "Hit him, then hold him until I can get there."

Anastasia laughed out loud. Sabrina skated toward them. Cal easily sidestepped her, caught her hand as she came around and pulled her close. He hadn't bothered with his skates yet, so she was nearly at eye level.

"I could take you out with one punch," she told him.

"You and what army?"

Amusement glinted in his brown eyes, amusement and something that called to her. Desire? That's what she wanted it to be, but she wasn't sure.

"Should I try to stand?" Anastasia asked, breaking the mood.

"It's a good place to start," Cal said, releasing Sabrina and moving to his daughter's side.

She rose to her feet and wobbled back and forth. Cal put his arm out and let her steady herself by holding on to him.

"Why don't you show her what to do," Cal said, glancing at Sabrina and smiling.

It didn't mean anything, she reminded herself. They'd always worked well as a team. That's all this was. Teamwork to help his daughter.

"In in-line skating, the key is to keep your center of gravity as low as possible," Sabrina said. "So skate with your knees bent. When you feel yourself losing your balance, the instinct is to reach up and back. That's just going to insure that you fall. Instead, drop into a crouch and bend forward."

She demonstrated the action.

"That's important to remember," Cal said. "You've got knee pads, elbow and wrist guards. If you fall forward, you're protected. If you fall backward, you're going to get bruised."

Anastasia looked doubtful but took a tentative step forward.

"Glide," Sabrina instructed. "Push out to the side, not forward."

"Come on, you can do it," Cal told his daughter. "I'll stay right with you."

It was a perfect summer afternoon, with the sky clear and the ocean sparkling just beyond the beach. Not that many people were out and they had a lot of room to practice. Anastasia was slow and off balance, but she managed to skate a few feet without holding on to her dad's arm.

She was tall and thin, still awkward, but Sabrina saw the hint of elegance in her carriage and facial bone structure. In just a couple of years, she was going to be a beauty. She was bright, sometimes too bright, and she was a survivor. All in all, Cal had done well with his daughter, and the young girl had gotten lucky with her father.

In the past few days, they'd started making peace with each other. They still had a lot of things to work out, and Anastasia wasn't going to be an easy teenager at times, but Sabrina knew they would form a bond that would last them forever. The love would be more precious for having been hard won.

When Anastasia could skate about a block without wobbling too badly, Cal put on his rented skates and joined them.

"Race you to the ice cream store," he said, pointing to a bright pink building up about two blocks away. "Winner has to buy."

"There's motivation not to win," Sabrina said, and laughed.

"You know I'm going to buy, anyway," he told her. "Where's your competitive spirit?"

"In my suitcase." She eyed his easy grace on the skates. While she could hold her own on a straight path, she wasn't the least bit athletic. Cal, on the other hand, could skate backward, do crossover turns and had, a few years before, spent a summer playing in a roller hockey league. His constant travel had forced him to drop out.

A warm breeze caressed them. Sabrina inhaled the scent of salt air and ocean and knew that whatever happened she would remember this time with Cal and his daughter.

"Dad!" Anastasia called as she realized the boardwalk had taken a slight dip and she was moving faster than was comfortable. "Help me."

Cal stood frozen in place, his expression wide with shock. "Catch her," Sabrina told him, and gave him a little push in his daughter's direction. She knew exactly why he was so stunned. She felt herself tearing up slightly as Anastasia plowed into her father.

The preteen probably didn't realize what she'd said, and if she did, she might get scared and embarrassed, only to retreat into sullen silence or rudeness. But she and Cal had heard it, had heard his daughter call him "Dad" for the first time.

Cal wrapped his arms around the girl. "Good going," he said, his voice gruff. "You're doing really well."

"Think so? It's fun. A little strange, but fun. Back in Ohio, a few kids had skates, but not that many. They're kind of expensive, aren't they?" She sounded wistful.

"If you want to start skating, I think we might be able to buy you a pair," he said. "I like skating. It could be something we do together."

Brown eyes met brown eyes. They were both a little scared, both wanting to reach out but terrified of rejection. Sabrina held her breath.

"Okay," Anastasia said shyly. "Can I get pink ones?"

Cal gave her a hug. "Sure. The brightest pink they have in the store. Maybe Day-Glo so you can put them on your bookshelf in your room and read by them instead of a lamp."

His daughter giggled.

"Now, what about that ice cream?" Cal asked. He looked at Sabrina. "I'll give you a head start."

"Five minutes," she called, and started skating.

"No way. A minute." His voice carried on the wind.

"Two," she yelled back, but it was too late. She

heard Cal starting out behind her. His stride was long and powerful and she knew she didn't have a chance.

"Dad, wait," Anastasia said, unable to keep up.

Sabrina glanced over her shoulder and winked. "Yeah, *Dad*, wait for your daughter."

He shrugged. "Can I help that I'm a sucker for the kid?"

"No, and I'm glad you can't."

"You're just excited about winning." With that he slowed and waited until Anastasia caught up with him.

Sabrina didn't bother racing ahead. She would rather they went together, so they moved up the boardwalk at the preteen's slightly awkward pace. On the way, they passed a couple of kids throwing a baseball back and forth.

Cal stared at them for a second. "You like baseball?" he asked. "There are two local pro teams here. One down here in Orange County, the other up in Los Angeles. I bet we could get tickets to a game."

They reached the ice cream stand. Anastasia sank onto a bench out front and sighed. "I've never been to a game. Is it fun?"

"You bet. There's hot dogs and peanuts still in the shell. This guy walks around the stand and tosses them to you."

Sabrina chuckled. "The game is fun, too."

"Oh, that," Cal said. "So you want to go?"

"Sure."

The girl smiled, and Sabrina realized for the first time that she'd inherited her smile from her father.

"Great. Okay, what flavor ice cream?" Cal asked as he fished a ten dollar bill out of his shorts pocket and started for the shop. "Sabrina, I know you like rocky road. On a cone, right?"

She nodded.

"Anastasia?"

"Chocolate, on a cone, too, please."

Sabrina raised her eyebrows. Please? That was a new one. Apparently the message about trying to be pleasant to make things easier had gotten through.

Cal returned in a couple of minutes and handed each of them their cones. He perched on the bench between the two females, his long legs pressing against Sabrina's. His free hand casually rested on her thigh, as if he'd done that a thousand times. As if he had the right. The heat from his fingers burned her skin. She thought about protesting, but the truth was, she liked him touching her, even if she didn't understand why he was doing it.

She wanted him. Lord help her, she also loved him. It was a deadly combination, and she didn't see a way for her to win in this situation. The most she could hope for was to entice Cal to her bed. For years she'd known he never thought of her as more than an employee and maybe a friend. But something had changed. She wasn't overly experienced, but she knew that while he'd been kissing her, he'd wanted her. Since then she'd caught him looking at her in a way that led her to believe he'd been thinking about her and their shared kiss as much as she had.

But then what? He might come to her bed and make love with her, but that would be the end of it. She knew Cal. He was loyal and faithful while he was interested, and then it was over. She didn't delude herself into thinking she might be the one woman on the planet who could actually figure out how to keep him around. The last thing she needed was to get her heart broken by him. She also didn't want to be used as a stand-in mom for Anastasia.

She had to be strong, she told herself. But when Cal told her she had a smudge of ice cream on her cheek, then brushed her skin to supposedly wipe it off, being strong seemed incredibly overrated.

Sabrina read the page for the third time, then put down her book. She wasn't getting anywhere in the story, and this was a new release by her favorite author. But today she couldn't concentrate. The phone sat next to her on the end table and she stared at it longingly. She'd sent out letters to the headhunters and had initial phone interviews. Both had promised to be in touch with her soon. So why weren't they calling her back? She needed to find out if there were jobs available to her. She had to get out of here before Cal drove her crazy.

It wasn't fair, she thought as she rose to her feet and crossed to the window. Anastasia and Cal had gone sailing for the afternoon, but she'd begged off. Privately she'd told Cal it would be good for him to have some time alone with his daughter. However, that was only part of the truth. The other part was she couldn't take much more of his attention.

In the past week...the seven days since their kiss...he'd been incredibly attentive. He was always close to her, touching her, smiling at her, flirting with her and generally going out of his way to make her feel special. She hated it. She loved it. She was slowly going insane.

Every part of her body was on fire. She couldn't look at him without wanting him. She had hormones pumping out chemicals that were leaving her edgy, while the voice of reason in her head kept screaming out warnings. The situation was intolerable and unlikely to get better anytime soon. If only...

She leaned her forehead against the sliding glass door and stared at the ocean. If only things could be different. Isn't that how it always went? If only her parents hadn't died. If only she could have kept from falling in love with her boss. If only she knew what to do with the rest of her life.

"We're back!"

The words were punctuated by the slamming of the door that led in from the garage. Sabrina quickly returned to the sofa and picked up her book. She forced herself to smile brightly. "Did you two have a good time?"

Cal flopped next to her on the sofa. "Great. The kid's a natural on the water."

Anastasia glowed. "I *love* sailing. Dad let me steer the boat and everything. We were going really fast and we tacked around this big cabin cruiser, but we're the sailboat so he had to give us the right of way and it was so cool!" She headed for the kitchen. "I'm going to get some water. Anybody else want anything?"

Sabrina tried to ignore Cal as he put his arm around her. "No, thanks," she said. His thumb brushed against her neck, the slow stroking igniting a passionate fire deep in her belly. "So you had fun?" she asked brightly.

"Uh-huh. She's really changed. I think she's starting to trust me."

"Oh, she is. It's wonderful to watch the two of you bond." The simple sentence was tough to get out because Cal had leaned close to press his lips against her throat. Her breath caught. "I don't think that's a good idea," she murmured.

"Why not? You like it. I can feel your pulse fluttering." He moved so that his mouth hovered over the hollow where her heartbeat gave away her aroused state.

"Anastasia will be back any minute." She tore herself away and pushed to her feet. "The baseball game's tomorrow," she said loudly so the girl could hear her. "Are you looking forward to it?"

Cal reached for her, but Sabrina managed to sidestep him. Anastasia walked back into the room.

"Sure," she said. "I think it will be fun." She took a sip from her glass, then moved to the sofa and plopped down next to her father. "I'm tired."

Cal ruffled her bangs. "Me, too, kid. You wore me out."

Anastasia giggled.

Sabrina watched them. Her heart ached. Not just from wanting Cal and being confused by what he was doing, but also because she was a bit player in a story that would never include her. Cal and his daughter were forming a family unit. She would always be the hired help. No matter how much she wanted it to be otherwise, she knew the truth. So it was better for everyone that she move on.

Oh, but it was going to hurt to go. She'd been in love with Cal for years and was only now admitting it. Even if it only took half that time to get over him, it was going to be a long while before she would be able to look at another man and not wish he was Cal Langtry.

Eleven

The phone call came early. As Cal rolled over to grab the receiver, he glanced at the clock. It was barely after five. "Yes," he said.

"Hey, boss, it's Griffin. Sorry to wake you up, but we got a problem with the Atlas rig."

Cal came instantly awake. He sat up in bed. "Explosion?"

"No, there was a fire. No one's hurt bad, but there are some injuries. We've got containment on the leak. No environmental damage. The media team is already gearing up to answer questions and there will be an investigation. I thought you'd want to know, is all."

Cal rubbed his eyes. "I'll get a plane out this morning," he said. There was a direct flight from the Orange County airport to Houston in a few hours. "I'll phone the office once I'm on board and give them my exact arrival time. The helicopter can meet me at the airport. I'll be on the rig by this afternoon."

"Sorry, boss. I know you're on vacation."

"Accidents happen. Hang tight, Griffin. I'll see you soon."

After hanging up, Cal stood and stretched. So much for the plans they'd made for the day.

A faint knock made him look up. Sabrina stood in the doorway. "I heard the phone," she said. "Is everything all right?"

Her hair was all mussed and her eyes were heavy with sleep. She wore an oversize cotton T-shirt that fell to mid-thigh. As she moved toward him, he was mesmerized by the sway of her breasts.

"There's a problem with the Atlas rig."

"An explosion?"

"Just a fire."

"Okay." She moved to the desk in his bedroom and picked up a pad of paper. After taking a pen, she walked to the bed and sat down. "What do you want me to do?"

What he wanted was for her to lie back and let him take her in his arms, holding her close as he kissed her all over, then strip her of her T-shirt and slowly make love to her.

Casually, so she wouldn't guess that the combination of her scanty attire, appealing body and his wayward thoughts were causing an obvious and predictable reaction, he slipped on his robe. For one thing, there wasn't time. He had to be at the airport in less than an hour. For another—

"Dad?"

Anastasia had only been calling him that for a couple of days, and every time she did, he felt a jolt of happiness in his heart.

"I heard the phone."

"It's all right," he said, and walked over to give her a hug. "There are a few problems with work. There was a fire on an oil rig."

She looked up at him. "That's bad, huh?"

"Very bad. It sounds like we were lucky, but I have to go make sure." He released his daughter and turned to Sabrina. "Call the airlines and get me on the seven o'clock flight to Houston. Griffin is supposed to make sure the helicopter is waiting for me, but double-check with Ada. I'll want to go directly to the rig.''

"You're leaving?'' Anastasia's voice was filled with outrage. "You can't leave. We've going to the baseball game tonight.''

Cal had forgotten. "I'm sorry to miss that, but I don't have a choice. I have a responsibility to the rig and my men. I have to be there to oversee everything. It's my job.''

Her eyes filled with tears. "You were lying about everything. I don't matter at all.''

"Anastasia, that's not right and you know it. I'll only be gone a couple of days. You and Sabrina can stay here and continue with your vacation. I'll be back before you know it,'' he said, but it was too late. She'd already run from the room.

Cal stared after her, torn between what he wanted to do and what he had to do. He glanced helplessly at Sabrina. She shrugged. "You're between a rock and a hard place, Cal. You're right about the rig. You *do* have a responsibility to your men. Unfortunately, the timing stinks. She's just starting to trust you, and from her point of view, you've just let her down. She'll understand in time.''

"How much time?''

"I don't know. This is hard for both of you. But you'll get through it. I just wish I could go with you.''

He'd known from the moment he received the phone call that Sabrina would have to stay with Anastasia, but he hadn't actually pictured himself making the trip without her. Except for a couple of vacations with girlfriends, Sabrina was always with him.

"I can manage on my own,'' he said lightly, knowing that what he was going to miss wasn't her efficiency, but her company.

"I know." She wrote a couple of more lines on the pad. "Okay, why don't you go shower and get dressed? In the meantime, I'll start the phone calls."

Twenty minutes later he walked into the kitchen to find Sabrina hanging up the phone. She looked up at him and smiled. "You're all set. The 7:00 a.m. flight to Houston. First class, window seat. The cab is on its way to take you to the airport." She handed him a cup of coffee. "I spoke to Ada. The helicopter will be waiting when you get off the plane." She pointed to a carry-on bag. "I packed you enough for three days. That should do it."

She still wore that damn T-shirt and virtually nothing else. He wanted her. Worse, at this moment, he felt like he needed her. He who had never needed anyone. And not just in his bed. Straight desire would have been a whole lot easier. The problem was, there wasn't anyone else he would trust to take care of Anastasia. He could deal with this crisis knowing his daughter was in good hands.

He glanced toward the stairs.

"I know what you're thinking," Sabrina said. "She'll be fine."

"I hate leaving her like this."

"I know."

"I looked in on her, but she was asleep, or at least pretending to be," he said. "Tell her goodbye for me and that I'm sorry about the game."

"I will."

Had her eyes always been that blue? he wondered as he put down the coffee and stepped toward her. Her skin looked so incredibly soft, and he had the strongest urge to touch her.

She swallowed. "Cal, the cab will be here in a couple of minutes."

"I know."

"I like working for you and I really don't want to—''

He pressed his mouth to hers. If she'd resisted, he would have stopped. Instead, she sighed and cupped his face. Her lips parted. He slipped his tongue inside, rediscovering the pleasure. Need mounted.

He rested his hands on her hips. Below the T-shirt, she wore panties and nothing else. Her breasts pressed into his chest. His groin tightened. He wanted her. Why hadn't he seen that before? How could he have worked with her all these years and not know?

Her arms came around him and she pulled him close. He angled his head so he could deepen the kiss. A faint sound distracted him. It was repeated.

She broke away. "The cab is here."

He cupped her cheek. "Take care of yourself. I'll call when I can."

She nodded.

He wanted to say something else, something significant that would let her know that even though he was leaving without her, she would be on his mind. But it was time to go and he couldn't find the words.

She walked him to the door. As the cab drove off, his last image was of Sabrina waving goodbye from the front porch of the rented beach house. An ache started in his chest. He had a bad feeling it wasn't going to go away until he was able to return to her.

Sabrina went upstairs to check on Anastasia. As Cal had suspected, the girl wasn't asleep. She sat up when

Sabrina walked into the room.

"Is he gone?" she asked, her voice sullen.

"Yes, although you didn't give him much of a send-off."

The girl shrugged. "He doesn't care. He promised to take me to the baseball game and he left, anyway."

Sabrina looked at her, at the mussed hair and pouting mouth. She didn't know whether to shake her or hug her. "This isn't about a baseball game, is it? You know the two of us are still going to go."

Anastasia flopped back on the bed. "I don't care what we do."

"Yeah, right. Like I'm going to believe that." She sat on the edge of the bed and took the girl's right hand in hers. "You know he cares about you. Having him leave is disappointing for everyone, but he doesn't have a choice. There are times in life when people have to take care of their responsibilities, even if they would rather be doing something else. You're old enough to know that."

Dark eyes met her gaze. "I know," she whispered. "It's just—" A single tear trickled down her temple.

Sabrina squeezed her fingers. "Oh, honey, why are you making this so hard? Cal wants to love you and take care of you. Just believe him. Stop looking for trouble where it doesn't exist."

The tears flowed faster. "What if he doesn't miss me while he's gone? What if he decides he doesn't want me anymore?"

Sabrina caught her breath. So they'd finally gotten to the reason behind Anastasia's actions. She hated that the preteen girl had so many doubts. She was at an age when life should be fun for her.

She opened her arms. "Come here." The girl sat up and Sabrina hugged her tight. "You know that's not going to happen. He's your father. No matter what, he'll always be your father. Trust him just a little. I promise he won't let you down."

Anastasia nodded. "I'll try."

Sabrina held on for a few minutes, then released her and brushed away her tears. "I have an idea. How about you and I try to get some sleep? Then after we get up, we'll have a girl day. We'll get our hair done, play with makeup, have dinner out, then head over to the game. What do you think?"

She smiled shyly. "I'd like that."

"Me, too." Sabrina kissed her forehead. "Go back to sleep." She rose and walked to the door. She knew that finding another job was the right thing to do, but leaving was going to be difficult. Before she'd just been worried about missing Cal, but now she had to worry about missing his daughter, as well.

Cal stretched out on the hotel room bed. It was late—too late to call—but he picked up the phone, anyway. The crisis was resolved and he would be heading back to California in the morning. His news could wait. Yet he needed to hear Sabrina's voice.

She answered on the third ring. "'Llo."

"I woke you."

He heard covers rustling, then she cleared her throat. "It's nearly one in the morning, of course you woke me. What did you expect?"

"I'm sorry. I should have waited."

"No, I wanted you to call. I turned off the other extension upstairs so you didn't wake Anastasia. How are you? How are things?"

He pictured her in that same T-shirt, lying on her back, the sheet pulled up to her shoulders. Ruffled hair, bare face, sleepy eyes. He got hard just thinking about it.

"I'm good. Everything is solved. We had a couple of mechanical problems, but the pumping is on schedule. The injuries were minor. The men are already out of the hospital. The other rigs are being checked, although I don't anticipate this happening again. I missed having you with me."

"Of course you did."

He heard the laughter in her voice and smiled. "I had to do all the work myself."

"Instead of having me at your beck and call. It must have been tough."

"I survived. Tell me about your day."

She chuckled. "You would have hated it. We went to a salon in one of the department stores and got the works. Hair, manicure, a new look with makeup."

Cal groaned. "You're right—I would have hated it. Hey, isn't she a little too young to be wearing makeup?"

"She's about the right age to start experimenting, and I don't think she'll be wearing it every day. But it was fun."

"My daughter is wearing makeup. Now I feel old."

"That's because you *are* old."

"Is this where I remind you that I sign your paychecks?"

"Actually, you don't. Franklin, your chief financial officer, signs the checks, or should I say, it's his signature stamp on them."

"You know what I mean."

Her voice was teasing. "Yes, boss, I know exactly

what you meant. I wasn't, however, very impressed with the argument. Oh, I should warn you, Anastasia cut her hair.''

"What?"

"Don't panic, she looks great. Actually it was her idea. We were both going to get a trim, but while we were waiting she looked through a few different books and picked out a couple of styles. We all talked about it and agreed on what would work. Her hair is shoulder length and she's got bangs. Actually her hair has a lot of curl and the shorter length shows that. She's already a beauty, Cal. You're going to have to fight off the boys with a stick.''

"I'm happy to do it," he growled. "Makeup and a haircut. I've had my baby girl for all of three weeks and she's already growing up too fast. I don't think I like that." He shoved a couple of pillows behind his head to get more comfortable. It was late and he should let Sabrina get back to sleep, but he didn't want to hang up. Not yet. "Tell me about the game.''

"It was fun. We beat them five to three. The seats were fabulous. We were close enough to admire the players' butts.''

"Tell me you didn't actually discuss that with my daughter.''

Sabrina laughed. "Of course not. She's too young to appreciate that sort of entertainment. But I did my share of looking, and let me tell you, it was very nice.''

"Hmm." He didn't like that, but he didn't feel he had the right to complain. Sabrina was his employee and friend, not his wife. She was allowed to look at all the butts she wanted, even though *he* only wanted her looking at his.

"We had hot dogs and peanuts, so we're full up with junk food. I'm sorry you had to miss it."

"Me, too. I'll make it up to you both, I promise."

"I know. Better, I think Anastasia knows it, too."

"Thanks for telling me that. You talked to her, didn't you?" he asked.

"Yes. She feels badly about what she did this morning. Sometimes she gets scared and acts without thinking. But she's better."

"I'm glad you're there with her. At least that part is familiar."

"I like her," Sabrina said. "She's a good kid. Although it was kind of strange to be left behind."

"I missed having you with me." He spoke without thinking, then realized it didn't matter. What he said was the truth. He *had* missed her.

"Oh, you did fine without me."

"That's not the point. I'm used to having you around."

He heard a faint sound, as if her breath had caught in her throat. He wanted to ask what she was thinking, but he didn't have the nerve. "I'm looking forward to being back with you both," he said, coming close to the point but still avoiding it.

"We're looking forward to having you back. Get some sleep, Cal. I'll call Ada in the morning and get the flight information, then Anastasia and I will be there to meet your plane."

"I'd like that. Thanks, Sabrina. 'Night."

"'Night."

After they hung up, Cal got undressed, then climbed back into bed. As he lay in the darkness he found himself thinking about his daughter. He'd spent so much of his life avoiding romantic entanglements, yet here he was, taking responsibility for a child. There was no going back with Anastasia. He couldn't take a couple of months to figure out if he liked the situation, then change his mind. He'd made a commitment and he was going to keep it.

The concept should have terrified him, but it didn't. He found himself looking forward to having her be a part of his life. He wanted to watch her grow up and become an adult. His only regret was all the time he'd already missed.

From there his mind drifted to Sabrina. He missed her, too, but in a different way. He wanted her in his bed, next to him. He wanted to feel her passion, to touch her and kiss her. He wanted to see her face change as passion overtook her. He thought about what it would be like to wake up next to her. Not just once, but a couple of times. Maybe with her, once he had her, he wouldn't be so eager to let her go.

"I see you eyeing those balloons," Cal teased.

His daughter grinned. "No way. I'm too old." But her gaze followed the balloon vendor as he made his way through the crowd at the fair.

"We'll get you one on the way out," Cal promised. "Because there's no way it would survive that!" He pointed ahead, to the small roller coaster that promised a wild ride unlike any ever experienced before.

Sabrina looked at the rickety track. "You two go ahead, because I'm not sure my life insurance policy is paid up."

Cal made several clucking sounds. "You're afraid," he said. "Sabrina's nothing but a chicken."

"Call me all the names you'd like, but I'm going to

sit right here.'' She pointed to a bench outside the entrance to the ride.

Anastasia grabbed his hand. ''Come on, Dad. It'll be great.''

He held back long enough to touch Sabrina's cheek. ''Are you sure you'll be all right by yourself?''

She smiled. ''I promise.'' She patted her stomach. ''I know we stopped at that deli for lunch a couple of hours ago, but it hasn't been long enough for me. If I went on that, I would toss my cookies, as they say. It wouldn't be pleasant for anyone close. I don't mind waiting. Really.''

''Da-ad!''

''I'm coming, I'm coming,'' he told his daughter. ''See you soon.''

Sabrina nodded as he was led away.

Twenty minutes later, he and Anastasia were soaring to the top of the track. From there he could make out the whole fairground. As it was midweek, the crowds weren't too large. They'd already been on most of the rides. Then the car slipped over the top of the track and everyone started to scream. He grinned.

''What do you think about going to the exhibit booths?'' he asked as he and Anastasia caught up with Sabrina. She handed them each a paper cone topped by a football-size serving of cotton candy.

''Sounds great,'' she said, and swiped a handful of the sticky confection.

''Sure,'' his daughter agreed. ''I don't care what we do. This is fun.''

Cal put his arms around the two females. Both moved closer to him. This was what he wanted, he realized, recognizing contentment, probably for the first time in his life. It wasn't flashy or something a lot of his friends or even his mother would understand, but it made sense to him. Anastasia and he had talked when he'd returned from his trip yesterday. She'd apologized for acting so badly, and he'd taken the time to explain why sometimes business would get in the way of their plans.

With Sabrina there'd been less to say. She understood about business because she was usually a part of it. What he couldn't tell her, or confess, was the thoughts he'd been having. Even today, at the fair, he felt like a kid on his first date. He'd found excuses to touch her and be close to her. A couple of times he'd even taken her hand and been thrilled when she hadn't pulled back.

Sabrina swiped another bit of the candy, then turned away. "Oh, look, a booth for frozen bananas."

"You're going to make yourself sick eating all this," he warned.

"I don't care. I don't get out to places like this much anymore. When I was growing up, we always went to the county fair and I loved it."

"You should see the Texas State Fair," Cal said. "It's huge."

"Yeah, yeah, everything is bigger in Texas. I keep hearing that, but have seen little proof."

"Is everything bigger there?" Anastasia asked.

"Well, little lady," Cal drawled. "I've been fixin' to talk to you about that."

His daughter giggled. "You talk funny. It's that accent. Kinda like a hick."

"A hick?" He pretended outrage and attacked her, tickling her and making her squirm and squeal.

"Daddy, no, stop!" She thrust her candy at Sabrina,

then used her free hands to push him away. "Stop tickling me. I'm not really ticklish."

Cal swooped her up and hugged her. "Yeah, brat, I can tell."

She wrapped her arms around his neck and squeezed. Cal felt an answering tightness in his chest, as if a band had just bound his heart. This young girl meant the world to him.

He turned and caught Sabrina's gaze. She smiled. "I told you so," she murmured.

She'd been right. About how wonderful it was to love a child.

Later, on the drive home, Anastasia fell asleep in the back seat. Cal checked on her in the rearview mirror, then reached over and took Sabrina's hand in his.

"I had a great time today," he said.

"Me, too. Coming to the fair was a lot of fun. I know Anastasia enjoyed it, and I'm sure it went a long way toward making up for your missing the baseball game."

"Sabrina…" His voice trailed off as he tried to figure out what to say. He wanted to invite her into his bed, or get an invitation into hers. "You've really helped me out these past few weeks and I'm grateful."

She gave him a quick smile. "No problem."

He cursed silently. *Smooth, Langtry, really smooth. You're making her sound like a housekeeper, not a lover.* "What I meant is—"

She pulled her hand free and rolled down the window.

"What's wrong?" he asked.

She shook her head. "I don't know. I don't feel that great. Are we almost back to the beach house?"

"Sure. About five more minutes."

"Good." She sucked in a deep breath.

Cal glanced at her as he drove down the dark streets. It was nearly ten and there wasn't that much traffic. As they neared the house, Sabrina moaned softly.

"I don't think I'm going to make it."

"Sabrina?"

She waved a hand at him. "Just drive. Please. Oh, God."

He pulled into the driveway and hit the button to release the garage door opener. She opened the passenger door and bolted for the house. Before he could go after her, Anastasia sat up.

"Daddy, I don't feel very good."

"Hold on, kitten, we're nearly there." He drove the car inside and turned off the engine. When he glanced back at his daughter, he was shocked to see her face was pale and coated with perspiration.

"I'm gonna be sick," she mumbled, then stepped out of car.

She made it as far as the trash can before throwing up.

Twelve

Cal hovered outside the bathroom door. He listened to the sound of running water. When it stopped, he tapped lightly.

"Sabrina? Are you all right?"

He heard a muffled groan. "No. Go away. I want to die in peace."

"I don't think you're going to die, I think you have food poisoning. Anastasia has it, too. She's been throwing up and feels pretty bad. As far as I can remember, the only thing you two ate that I didn't was the potato salad we got from the deli. I guess it had been left out too long."

"I guess."

He heard a thud. "Sabrina? What's going on?"

"Nothing. I'm just sitting here on the floor waiting until the next time I have to puke my guts out. Or deal with whatever is left in my system leaving the other way. I know, I know, more information than you wanted. Go worry about your daughter. I'll die quietly. Tell my family I want a simple funeral and I don't want them wearing black."

"How about a catered lunch?"

"Oh, God, don't mention food."

"Sorry." He pressed his hand against the door. "When you feel better, let me know and I'll get you something to drink. I don't want you getting dehydrated.''

"Just go check on Anastasia, Cal. I have to be sick now and I'd like to do that in private.''

"I'll be back.''

"I'll try to get excited about that fact.''

He moved down the hall and into his daughter's room. She lay on the bed, her face pale, her eyes dark with suffering. "Daddy, I feel terrible.''

"I know, honey. You've got food poisoning. It'll take a few hours, then the bad food will be gone and you'll start to perk up.'' He pointed to the glass of water on her nightstand. "Have you been drinking?''

She shook her head. "It's too hard.''

"Anastasia.'' He sat next to her and pulled her into his arms. She leaned against him, her body limp and trusting. "Come on. Just a couple of sips. Okay?''

She nodded.

He held the glass and she sipped. When she was done, she pushed it away and leaned her head against his chest. He put down the drink.

"You're going to be fine,'' he promised as he got more comfortable on the bed and stroked her hair.

"How come you're not sick?''

"I didn't eat what you did. Which is good. Someone has to take care of you two.''

"Sabrina got it, too?''

"Uh-huh. Right now she's in the bathroom threatening to die.''

Anastasia raised her head and looked at him. Her expression turned stricken. Cal instantly realized his mistake. He kissed her forehead. "Sorry, honey. That was a stupid thing to say. Sabrina's fine. She's not going to die. She feels pretty bad right now, but in a couple of hours, she'll be able to get some sleep, and by morning, it will all be over. I promise."

"I don't want her to die."

"I know. I'm sorry I said that. It was supposed to be funny."

She nodded. "I don't want you to die, either."

"I'm not going to."

"Promise?"

He made an X on his chest. "I'll do everything I can to stay alive so I can be with you. We have a lot of time to make up for."

Anastasia rubbed her eyes and looked at him. "Am I bad for liking you?"

"No. Of course not. Why would you think that?"

"I just—" She shrugged. "My other parents. I still miss them so much, and I want them to come back, but I know they're really gone forever." Her brown eyes filled with tears.

He cupped her face and brushed away the tears. "Anastasia, you've had more than your share of heartache, haven't you? You're confused about all of this and I can't blame you. I'm the grown-up and I get confused, too. Your parents, the ones who adopted you, will always be your Mom and Dad. You love them." He touched the spot just below the hollow in her throat. "They'll live in your heart."

"Sometimes it's hard to remember them."

"Do you have a picture of them?"

"Yeah. Two."

He stuffed the second pillow behind his head. "Do you like looking at the photos?"

She nodded.

"Then keep them out on your dresser. I won't mind. I want you to remember them. When you're feeling better, I'd like you to tell me about them. They took care of you when I didn't know about you. I'm grateful that they were good people and that they loved you. That's what I would have wanted if I couldn't have been there myself. I'm glad you love them.''

She glanced at him. ''Sabrina says it's okay to love lots of people.''

''That's true.''

''They won't be mad?'' she asked in a whisper.

''If there's a little girl in heaven with no one to look after her, will you be mad if they take care of her for a while?''

Anastasia thought about that one. ''They'll still love me, right?''

''Of course.''

''Then I wouldn't mind. It's scary to be alone.''

Cal thought about his life. He knew that demon personally. ''You're not alone anymore.''

Anastasia rested her head on his shoulder. ''I know, Daddy. I have you and I have Sabrina.''

He stroked her back. Somehow he'd gotten lucky with his daughter. He didn't know what he'd done to deserve having her in his life, but he was damn grateful she'd shown up.

She sat up suddenly. ''Daddy, I'm gonna be sick again.''

''All right, honey. I'll carry you to the bathroom.''

But as he reached for her, he was too late. Anastasia threw up over him, the sheets, the blankets and herself. When she was finished, she burst into tears.

''It's no big deal,'' he said, and picked her up. After carrying her into the bathroom and leaving her with orders to get out of her dirty clothes and put on a clean nightgown, he stripped off his shirt and snagged another before returning to her bedroom. It was a mess. He glanced at the clock. Nearly nine. He had a feeling it was going to be a long night.

Cal finished filling the dishwasher. There were bowls from the soup he'd made for Anastasia and Sabrina, not to mention plates from toast and pots from his own food. It was nearly three in the afternoon. As he'd suspected, he hadn't gotten a lot of sleep the night before. Anastasia had made steady trips to the bathroom, although after that one accident, she'd managed to make it on time. Sabrina had retreated to her bedroom about midnight and, to the best of his knowledge, was feeling better. She'd spent the morning lying low.

When he'd finished in the kitchen, he went upstairs to check on his daughter. Anastasia lay curled up on her side, asleep. She'd taken a shower early that afternoon and had asked him to change the sheets. Which reminded him—they were still in the washer.

On the way to the laundry room, the phone rang. He picked up the receiver. "Hello?"

"Mr. Langtry, good afternoon. This is Ada, Sabrina's assistant. I hope I'm not interrupting."

"Not at all." Cal carried the remote into the laundry room off the garage. He moved the wet sheets from the washer to the dryer and pressed the Start button. "What can I do for you, Ada? Is there another crisis?"

He grimaced. If there was, this time he was going to have to get someone else to take care of it. He needed to be here.

"Not really."

He frowned. "Ada, something's wrong. I can hear it in your voice."

She cleared her throat. "Nothing's wrong. It's

just..." What he heard sounded suspiciously like a strangled laugh. "You received a phone call a few minutes ago. From a magazine editor. She didn't want to give me the information, but when I told her you were on vacation and couldn't be reached, she agreed to tell me what she wanted. I said I would relay the information to you so you could get in touch with them."

A suspicion arose in his mind but he refused to voice it. "What is it about this time?" he asked instead, hoping it wasn't what he was afraid it was.

"It's certainly unique. Are you familiar with *Prominence Magazine*?"

"Of course." Damn, he'd forgotten all about them and their silly World's Most Eligible Bachelor story. "But I don't think I'm their style." It was true—at that very moment, he felt anything but "eligible."

"On the contrary, Mr. Langtry," Ada continued, her amusement more evident now. "You appear to be exactly their style. You see, they're doing a year-long series of articles on, well, bachelors. The world's most eligible bachelors, to be exact. And you're one of the twelve."

Cal tried not to sound annoyed...or embarrassed. "Just my luck. I was hoping they would forget all about me."

"You knew?" Ada's surprise overwhelmed her amusement for just a moment. "But I just got the faxed information now. How did you know?"

"They contacted me a couple of weeks ago. When I called to tell them I wasn't interested, the editor somehow convinced me to do an interview."

"And a photo shoot."

"They want pictures?" Cal didn't think it could get much worse.

"Yes, sir. I understand there's going to be a large spread in each issue. I think you're Mr. June!"

He swore under his breath. Mr. June? He didn't want to think about the board's reaction to any of this. They would tease him for months.

"Anything else?" he asked.

"No, that's it."

"Go ahead and scan the fax into my computer, so I can access it later. I'll call them in a few days. Thanks for letting me know."

"Mr. Langtry, it was my pleasure."

He thought about how quickly word would spread in the office. "I'll just bet it was," he said, and couldn't help smiling ruefully. If this were happening to anyone but him, he would get a big kick out of it, too.

He returned the remote to its base, then climbed the stairs to check on his daughter. She was still sleeping soundly. So far she hadn't been sick that day and she was keeping down fluids, so she seemed to be on the mend. He made his way to Sabrina's room and knocked on the door.

"Come in," she called.

He stepped inside. She sat up in bed, reading a book. She, too, had showered earlier that afternoon. She wore a different oversize T-shirt and no makeup. In the afternoon light, she looked like a kid.

"How do you feel?" he asked.

"A lot better."

He motioned to the tray on the dresser. She'd finished off a large bowl of soup and some toast. "You're eating well. If I didn't know better, I would say you've been faking it."

She fluttered her eyelashes. "Not me. Why would I want to do something like that?"

"Oh, I don't know," he said as he settled on the edge of her bed. "Maybe to force me to take care of Anastasia so we could bond some more."

"What a clever idea," she said, still all innocence. "But you're giving me way too much credit. I wish I'd thought of that, but I didn't."

He leaned forward and touched his index finger to her nose. "Liar."

"Me? Lie? Never. I might not have been as sick as Anastasia, and I'll admit that I've stayed in bed even though I'm probably well enough to get up, but I didn't fake it." Her mouth twisted. "I spent way too much of last night barfing my guts up."

He winced. "There's an attractive visual. Thanks for sharing."

"Anytime. So how's it going?"

"Anastasia is fine. She's weak, but eating a little, and she's able to keep it down. Right now she's asleep." He cleared his throat. "Whether or not you planned it, we've bonded. We talked about her parents, the ones who adopted her. She's concerned about divided loyalties. I explained that it was okay to care about them and me." He frowned. "At least I tried to make that clear."

"Cal, I'm sure you did great. You have to trust yourself with this stuff. I'm really impressed with how well you're doing. You're a natural at being a dad."

He appreciated the confidence, even if he wasn't so sure it was deserved. There were still many things he didn't understand. "I like that she calls me that. Dad, I mean."

"I thought you might."

"It's strange how much that means to me."

She put her book aside and pulled her knees to her chest. "I don't think so. She's your daughter and you're learning to care about her. It's only natural you want her to care back. People tend to get nervous when they put their heart on the line, but the other person doesn't."

He knew what she meant. He had the same type of concerns with his relationship with her. Except he wasn't putting his heart on the line. Wanting wasn't the same as loving. But he did *care*. He'd always liked Sabrina.

As a friend, he reminded himself. Which was different from wanting her. Now he had both feelings to wrestle with. There didn't seem to be any easy answers.

"I haven't loved anyone in a long time," he admitted. "Not since Tracey and I were kids and I loved her."

"You love your parents," she told him.

"Maybe." He shrugged. "Probably. If you can love someone without forgiving them for what they've done."

"You mean keeping Janice's pregnancy from you?"

"That and letting Anastasia be adopted when Janice died. To me, that's unforgivable. I might reconsider if my mother showed any interest in her granddaughter, but I know that's never going to happen."

Sabrina looked unhappy. "I want to disagree with you, but I can't. I don't see her coming around, either. It's a difficult situation. The good news is that you have

Anastasia with you now.'' She stretched. "Is there any news from the office?"

Cal thought about his call from Ada.

Sabrina raised her eyebrows. "Wow, what is it? I don't think I've ever seen that particular expression on your face before. An odd combination of embarrassment, resignation and—" She peered at him. "What's that last emotion? Amusement?"

"You look tired. I should let you get some rest."

He started to stand. Sabrina leaned forward and grabbed his arm, then pulled him back onto the bed. "No, you don't. Obviously this is very interesting, and I want you to start at the beginning. Tell me everything and speak slowly."

Cal hadn't minded when Ada had first mentioned that *Prominence Magazine* had called, but now, sitting next to Sabrina, he felt himself flushing. "It's nothing."

"You couldn't be more wrong." She shifted until she'd tucked her legs under her. "Come on, Cal. You can tell me anything. We don't have many secrets from each other."

He wondered what her secrets were. What did she think about that she didn't want him to know? A couple of weeks ago he would have said he didn't have any secrets from her. She knew the worst about him and still kept coming back, which was one of the reasons he liked her so much.

"Ada called," he admitted. "*Prominence Magazine* is trying to get in touch with me."

Sabrina clapped her hands together. "They want to do an article? That's great!"

He cleared his throat. "Not exactly."

"Then what?"

"Apparently they're doing a special series. The World's Most Eligible Bachelors or something like that. I've been chosen for one of the months. You know, sort of as the bachelor of the month."

Sabrina could be annoying, stubborn and argumentative, but she rarely disappointed him. This was no exception.

She stared at him blankly for two seconds, then started to laugh. "Bachelor of the month?" she asked, then continued laughing when he nodded.

The hearty chuckles filled the room. She clutched her stomach and rolled onto her side. "Oh, Cal."

He wrestled with mild annoyance. "What seems to be so funny? I'm wealthy, single, and there are those who think I'm decent-looking."

She could only gasp for air. "I can't stand it. Are they going to run a profile, complete with statistics and a post office box so you can get fan mail?"

"I don't know, but if you keep this up much longer, I'm going to make you answer all the fan mail and send back a picture with the response."

She coughed and raised herself up on one elbow. Her face was flushed, her eyes damp from tears. "Oh, my. I haven't laughed like that in far too long. I work for one of the world's most eligible bachelors, huh? So how have I managed to escape falling for your charms all these years?"

She'd been teasing him, so he teased her back. He touched her cheek. "I'm not so sure you have."

Instead of bursting out into more laughter, Sabrina froze. Her blue eyes widened as she stared at him. "I don't know what you're talking about."

But the disclaimer came too late. Her shock had been

genuine, as had the flash of guilt. She *had* kept secrets, and one of them was about him.

He didn't know what exactly she felt about him. For all he knew she'd wrestled with a crush for the first couple of days she'd worked for him but had recovered nicely. But he hoped it was more.

"Sabrina."

"No!"

She started to scramble off the bed. He caught her and pulled her against him.

"Wait. We need to talk about this," he said.

"There's nothing to say."

One of his hands rested on her hip. Her T-shirt had pulled up to her waist and he was touching the place where her silky panties ended and bare skin began. She pushed at his chest.

"Cal, I don't—"

"Yes, you do," he said, cutting her off. "We both do. We have for a while. I want to kiss you."

She shuddered as if he'd threatened her. Maybe he had.

"Sabrina, I—"

She cupped his face in her hands. "So do it."

"What?"

"Kiss me."

Thirteen

There wasn't a doubt in her mind as to where this was heading. Sabrina wished she could find the backbone to be strong, to resist Cal and his passion, but it wasn't going to happen. At least not today. She'd wanted him—*loved him*—for far too long. She knew the pitfalls, the fact that he would quickly grow tired of her. She knew that he would break her heart without ever once having a clue as to her feelings. Maybe it was better for that to happen. At least when the time came, she would be motivated to leave. But for now...there was this moment and the magic she felt in his arms.

He kissed her gently, yet thoroughly, brushing his mouth back and forth against hers, as if he had to convince her to cooperate. She thought about pointing out the fact that kissing had been her idea to begin with, but that would mean speaking. She didn't want to do anything that would separate his mouth from hers. Not when keeping them joined felt so incredibly right.

She parted her lips in anticipation of him deepening the kiss, and he didn't disappoint her. His tongue moved inside, exploring, perhaps remembering. She met him, and they stroked each other. The sensations were more intense than she recalled. More perfect. This was Cal, this was who and what she'd always wanted. Even if she'd wanted to resist him, she no longer had that option.

In his effort to keep her from getting off the bed, he'd grabbed her and pulled her close. She straddled one of his thighs, his hands resting on her waist, hers clutching his shoulders. Her breasts hovered close to his chest without touching. She could feel her nipples getting hard, and that secret place between her legs getting wet.

"Sabrina," he murmured as he moved his hands up and down her back. "You are incredible."

The words washed over her like a caress. For today, for this moment, she would believe him, because she wanted to. She wasn't foolish, in fact she rarely did anything without weighing the consequences. So she was due for an afternoon of not thinking. While in his arms, she would only feel.

He raised his arms and used his right index finger to trace a line from her forehead, down her nose to her mouth. "Hold that thought," he said.

She stared at him. "What?"

"I need you to hold that thought. I want to go check on Anastasia to make sure she's asleep, and I want to get something from my room." His dark eyes burned with passion and intensity. "I know it's a risk leaving right now. Don't you dare change your mind."

Then he was gone. Sabrina stared after him. He'd left her? Just like that? She slid off the bed and started toward the door.

Some of the need and the desire faded. Maybe it was a good thing, she thought. Maybe she should come to her senses. This was her boss, after all. Yes, she was planning on quitting her job, but she hadn't yet. How was she supposed to face him tomorrow? As far as career planning went, this was *not* an intelligent move.

The half-closed door opened and Cal stepped back

inside. He took one look at her face, crossed to her and pulled her hard against him. "Uh-oh, I knew it would be a mistake to leave you. Unfortunately, I didn't have a choice." He kissed her until she was once again weak in his arms. He slowly withdrew from the kiss and murmured, "The good news is Anastasia is fast asleep. We're also protected."

He pulled something out of his jeans pocket and tossed it on the nightstand. Sabrina looked at the small square package. He'd gone to get a condom.

She swallowed. Should she be pleased that he wanted to take care of her or horrified that she hadn't thought of that herself?

She pushed away from him and sank onto the edge of the bed. "I'm way too out of practice to be doing this with you."

Cal crouched in front of her. "What does that mean?"

He looked so handsome and so damned earnest. How was she supposed to resist him? His mouth was still damp from their kisses. She touched his lower lip and a thrill shot through her. Was it so wrong to want to make a few memories? Realistically she knew they were all she was going to be taking with her. Memories to get her through the night. Would she rather be able to look back on how it was once, knowing she could never have it again, or would she rather just wonder how it might have been?

She traced his eyebrows, then his mouth. He touched her finger with the tip of his tongue and she was lost. Better to know, she thought. Better to remember than to wonder.

She leaned forward and kissed him. Keeping his mouth firmly against hers, he rose to his feet, pulling her along with him. They pressed together from shoulders to thighs. He was strong and broad, all hard muscles and lean lines. His arousal lay against her stomach. Her throat tightened slightly as she leaned in a little more so she could feel all of that part of him. She loved knowing he wanted her. She still wasn't sure what had changed his mind or why he suddenly found her attractive, but the physical proof of his desire couldn't be ignored.

"Sweet Sabrina," he murmured against her mouth.

He cupped her head, then moved one hand down her back. On the return trip, he went under her T-shirt and stroked the bare skin at the small of her back. She shivered. Her whole body felt tingly, as if a million tiny bubbles floated through her bloodstream.

There were too many sensations. How wonderful he tasted. The warm, wet stroking of his tongue against hers. The ache of her breasts as they flattened against his chest. His strong fingers tracing an ever-smaller circle on her back, the dampness between her thighs, the hard ridge of his need. It was too much. It wasn't enough. She flexed her hips against him.

He broke the kiss, swore softly and pressed his forehead against hers. "When I was about sixteen or seventeen, I used to get into trouble when I kissed girls. About an hour of passionate making out and I would—" He shrugged. "Lose control. They didn't have to be touching me. It just happened."

Their breath mingled. His hands tugged at the hem of her shirt and she wanted him to just pull it off.

"I don't understand what that has to do with this."

He smiled. "Just that I'm in danger of that happening now. It's one thing at seventeen. It's quite another at thirty-four."

Dear Lord, she wanted to believe him. She wanted to think that she could turn him on that much. It wasn't true, of course. He was just being kind. But it was so sweet of him.

"Thank you," she whispered.

He glared at her. "Thank you? That wasn't a gift, Sabrina. It was the truth. I want you so damn much."

He clutched her upper arms and pulled her hard against him. His grip was nearly unforgiving and she grabbed him back, just as hard. Their kiss was intense, a sensual assault of lips and tongues. The passion built, as did the heat. A whimper caught in the back of her throat.

"Please," she managed to say against his mouth.

"I want you," he told her. "More than you can imagine."

He released her and jerked the hem of his polo shirt out of his jeans. With one strong, fluid motion, he pulled it up and over his head.

Sabrina stared at his bare chest, at the dark hair forming an inverted triangle, at the sculpted beauty of his muscles. She'd seen his chest before, of course. But seeing it from a slight distance was very different from having it right in front of her. This time, she was allowed to touch.

She placed her hands on his shoulders and let his heat seep into her. Then she moved her hands down...slowly...very slowly. The hair was a cool and ticklish contrast to his skin. Muscles rippled under her touch. She stroked up a little, then continued the journey, pausing to let her fingertips trace tiny circles on his nipples.

Instantly the two points hardened. He caught his

breath. "Is that what it feels like when you're touched there?" he asked.

She looked at him. "What do you mean?"

"It feels great. If I'd known what it was going to be like, I would have requested it sooner." At her continuing confusion he shrugged. "No one's ever touched me there...like that before."

Sabrina felt a thrill of satisfaction. She'd worried about measuring up to the other women is his life. She didn't consider herself ugly, but she wasn't an eighteen-year-old, either. Cal seemed to prefer spectacular women, and she was simply average.

But maybe it wasn't just about appearance. She had other things to offer, apparently things those women hadn't thought of.

She flicked her nail over the taut peaks. "So you like it."

"Yes, I—"

She bent forward and kissed him there, then stroked her tongue against his skin. He swore under his breath and jerked hard. "You're determined to make me embarrass myself, aren't you?"

"Of course not. Although I wouldn't mind if you did."

"No. I want this to be great for both of us."

He touched a finger to her chin and drew her upright. When she had straightened, he turned her gently until she had her back to him.

"Stay still, just like that," he murmured, then kissed the nape of her neck.

Shivers rippled down her spine, and goose bumps erupted on her arms. He moved to the curve by her ear, tracing it to the neckline of her T-shirt, then up to her jaw. His warm breath contrasted with the dampness his open-mouthed kisses left behind.

Strong hands rested on her hips. He moved them around and up, sliding from her waist to her ribs to her breasts. He hovered slightly below for a few seconds. She tensed in anticipation. Her breathing increased; she felt her nipples harden. The ache intensified. She *needed* him to touch her or she wouldn't survive.

"Cal," she breathed.

"What, lover?"

"I..."

"Tell me."

"I can't." She didn't dare say the words. What if he changed his mind?

"Tell me what you want. Or if that's too hard, show me." He stepped closer and brushed his arousal against her derriere. "You have proof that I want you. I'd like to know the same."

At first she thought he was teasing. She spun toward him, determined to scold him for playing at a time like this. But when she saw his face, she knew he wasn't kidding. Doubt flickered in his eyes. The fire nearly hid it from view, but she knew him well enough to sense he was serious.

If he'd wanted to reassure her, he couldn't have picked a better way. Knowing that he was also a little nervous about the whole thing made her own self-doubts much easier to bear.

"Is this different?" she asked. "Am I different from the other women?"

"Of course. They were just people I dated for a while. But you and I—" He shrugged. "I *like* you." As if liking was significant. Maybe it was.

"Oh, Cal, you are the most difficult man." She

cupped his face and raised herself up on tiptoes so she could press a kiss to his mouth. "Yes, I want you. Better now?"

"Some." His expression turned wicked. "I'd like proof."

She thought about the hard points of her nipples. He could see them through the thin cotton of her T-shirt. But there was other, more graphic proof. Her panties had been wet from their first kiss. Did she dare?

This was, she reminded herself, Cal. She doubted there was anything she could do to shock him. They would have only this one time together. Maybe it was time to let go, to just experience the moment.

She took his hand in hers and drew it to her belly. She slid his fingers lower beneath her panties until he tangled in the red curls. She was wet and swollen. There was no way he could miss the signs of her arousal.

He didn't. When he touched her there, he sucked in his breath. "You feel great," he murmured, then lowered his mouth to hers.

While they kissed and his tongue brushed against hers, his fingers provided a sensual counterpoint below. He explored her, discovering secret places, the tiny bud of pleasure, the waiting heat that would soon welcome him. He dipped inside, going deep, then rubbed against the slick walls. He circled the swollen knot so gently and so perfectly she made a half cry, half moan in the back of her throat. Her thighs trembled, her knees buckled and she had to lean against him to keep standing.

He tore his mouth away. "I can't believe how much I want you," he said, then picked her up and set her on the bed.

Before she could lie back, he tugged her T-shirt over her head and pulled off her panties. She didn't have time to be embarrassed. Even as the first self-conscious thoughts formed, Cal was reaching for his belt. To be completely honest, she admitted she was far more interested in seeing him naked than she was concerned about him seeing her.

He kicked off his shoes, then pushed down his jeans and briefs in one quick movement. As he bent to pull them off completely, he also removed his socks.

And then he was naked. Tall, lean, powerful and very male. She reached for him. He grabbed her wrist. "You can't," he said. "I swear I'll explode if you touch me there."

She tilted her head and pretended genuine concern. "You know, Cal, I've read some articles and I understand there are some techniques that can be used to help with that problem."

He drew his dark eyebrows together. "I don't have a problem."

"I know it's difficult for a man to admit that everything isn't perfect in the bedroom, but sometimes—"

He lunged for her. She tried to scramble away, but he was quicker. Before she reached the far side of the bed, he had a hold of her ankle and was steadily pulling her back.

"Cal! No! Stop!" she said between giggles.

She tried to kick him, then realized they were both naked and she was exposing herself in ways she normally tried to avoid.

He knelt on the bed, flipped her over, then straddled her thighs. "So I have a problem, do I?"

The promise of retribution in his eyes made her

squirm. "No. I don't know what I was thinking. You're perfect. Really."

"Uh-huh. Sure. You say that now."

He tickled her ribs. She wiggled and twisted, all the while laughing and trying to catch hold of his hands to make him stop.

"Cal—"

She had to gasp for breath. He grinned down at her. "You are so beautiful," he said.

The unexpected compliment took away the last of her air. She couldn't do anything when he encircled her wrists, raised her arms and pinned her hands above her head. Then she didn't care because he leaned over and kissed her.

"I have ultimate power," he said, moving his chest gently over her nipples and making her gasp with pleasure. "Say it, Sabrina."

He was laughing, but at that moment it was completely true. "You have ultimate power."

"I know." He released her hands and cupped her face. "But you have a lot of power, too."

"Just not ultimate?"

"Sorry, no."

She hadn't known it would be like this. That the teasing in their regular relationship would spill over into bed. That she would enjoy not just the lovemaking, but the connection.

"So, you *are* a natural redhead. I'd wondered."

She blinked while his comment sank in. Then she felt herself blushing hotly. "Cal!"

He flashed her another wicked grin, then lowered his head to her left breast. As his mouth closed over her nipple, she sighed. If him thinking he had ultimate power meant she got to feel this good, she didn't mind at all.

His mouth was wet and warm as he caressed her. He moved his hand to touch her other breast, his fingers mimicking the movement of his tongue. He flicked over the taut bud and she felt the fire shoot down to her thighs. She arched into him. In response, he began to move his hips. As he still straddled her thighs, that most male part of him rubbed against her nest of curls. Close, but not touching that most sacred place, the contact aroused and frustrated in equal measures.

She rolled her head from side to side, not sure how much of this she could stand. She ran her hands up and down his back, then wove her fingers through the silky strands of his hair. She could feel herself getting more and more wet as her body prepared itself for the ultimate release.

He raised his head and looked at her. Passion darkened his eyes. "I want you," he said. "All of you."

"Yes, Cal. I want that, too."

He shifted off of her, urged her to part her legs, then knelt between them. He put his hands on her ankles and slowly slid his fingers up, taking his time, making her wait. The slow, sensual stroking made her quiver inside. She clutched at the blankets and held back a whimper.

When he'd completed the journey, he brushed his thumbs against her curls. As he had just a few minutes before, he touched close, but not *there*. She thought she might die from needing him so much.

"Sabrina," he murmured, then lowered his head. He pressed a kiss to her belly. His thumbs parted the delicate folds of her femininity, exposing her to him, then he gave her the most intimate kiss of all.

The first touch of his tongue nearly drove her off the mattress. She drew her heels toward her rear and bent her knees. Every muscle tensed. He circled the special spot, getting close, but not pressing directly on it. Tension increased, as did her breathing.

A part of her disconnected enough to look at the situation. She'd always wondered what Cal would be like in bed. After all, he was single, good-looking and rich. For most women, he would just have to show up and they would be happy. But he wasn't like that. He took his time pleasing her. She could tell he was experimenting with different touches, trying to see which she enjoyed the most.

She felt herself building toward release and she wanted to hold back. Not just because she was enjoying what he was doing, but also because she wasn't sure she was ready to let him witness her loss of control. There was something frightening about being that exposed to a man. No, she thought. There was something frightening about being that exposed to Cal. It was specifically about him. If she gave in—he would see her soul. After that, when he walked away, she would be in that much more pain. So maybe she wouldn't let herself go all the way. Maybe she would hold back.

As plans went, it was a good one…in theory. Then Cal turned his attention to the tiny button. He rubbed it lightly but quickly and she began to spiral out of control. When he gently inserted a finger and pressed up from the inside, as if to caress her from both sides, she lost the ability to reason, or remember why she was trying to hold back. There was only the magic she felt and the onward pressing for release.

When it flashed through her, she wasn't prepared. The exquisite pleasure captured her and flung her around, filling her, buffeting her, tossing her into the air, before letting her float gently back into reality. As her body stopped trembling and the soft cries died in her throat, she found herself in Cal's arms.

A thousand thoughts crowded in. She was embarrassed by her vigorous reaction to what he'd done. If she'd had to come, couldn't she have done so quietly and with dignity? She wanted to know what he was thinking, and if he was turned on by what had happened, and she was really dying to know if he was still hard, but she didn't dare look.

He touched her mouth. "You are so amazing," he said quietly. "I felt so connected to you that I almost lost it."

As he spoke, she felt the nudging against her thigh that told her he was still aroused, and if the light in his eyes was anything to go by, more than ready to have his way with her.

"Thank you," she whispered.

He smiled. "No, Sabrina. Thank *you*."

He slipped on his protection, then moved back between her legs. She was slick, but he still stretched her as he entered her body. When he braced his hands on either side of her shoulders, she looked at him. He met her gaze and began to move.

It was something she'd never done before. She'd never made love while looking into the eyes of her partner. The intimacy terrified her, but she couldn't look away and she wasn't going to be the first one to close her eyes.

The pressure built, as did the promise of another release. Cal moved slowly at first, then faster, building a rhythm that matched their need. His expression tightened. She felt him getting closer. That knowledge drew her along with him and she clutched at him.

"I can't hold back," he breathed.

"I'm right with you."

He stiffened and moaned. "Sabrina!"

"Yes."

Her body convulsed around him, pulling him in. She drew her knees back and arched her hips, taking all of him.

And still they looked at each other. She saw the fire in his eyes, the moment of perfect pleasure, the easing of tension, the half smile of a satisfied male.

He rolled onto his side and pulled her against him. As he held her close, he stroked her back and her hair. She sighed in contentment.

"Who knew?" he asked, his voice low and lazy.

Who indeed, she thought.

Cal woke as the first hint of light appeared at the edge of the blinds. He glanced at the clock, but it was barely six, so there was no need to get up and return to his own bed just yet. He had a little time.

He shifted so that he could turn and watch Sabrina as she slept next to him. Her short red hair was mussed. The sheet and light blanket had slipped enough to expose one bare shoulder and her arm. She looked sexy and adorable and he found himself wanting her again.

Cal grinned. He had to admit, he'd impressed himself. A couple of times the first night wasn't that unusual. After all, it had been a while and he was with someone new. But sometime after midnight, when they'd been doing nothing more erotic than talking about business, he'd found himself hard and desperate for her. Fortunately, Sabrina hadn't taken much convincing.

In the privacy of his mind, he was willing to admit he'd been terrified. After they'd made love for the first time yesterday afternoon, he'd left her room. Anastasia joined them for dinner, although she and Sabrina hadn't had much to eat. But when his daughter retired for an early evening, Cal hadn't known what to do. He'd wanted to spend the night with Sabrina. Not just to make love with her, but to enjoy time with her, too.

He'd hovered in the hallway, not sure of his reception. He'd been thrilled when she'd opened her door to come looking for him.

They were good together, he thought, as he resisted the urge to stroke her face. He wanted to touch her, but she needed her sleep. He hadn't given her much chance for rest last night. And there would be plenty more time for them later.

He quietly got out of bed and reached for his clothes. After pulling on jeans, he made his way to his room where he showered and dressed. As he shaved, he thought about Sabrina and wondered when the familiar restlessness would strike. It usually happened right after he'd been with a woman. By the second or third time they were together, he was already fighting the need to get away.

But he didn't feel anything like that this morning. He only wanted to be with Sabrina more. He could imagine waking up next to her for a while. He put down the razor and rubbed his face. What did that mean? Was it different because he'd known her for so long? Because he already liked and respected her? Or was it something specifically about being with Sabrina? Chemistry? Or fate?

Three hours later he still didn't have any answers, but as Anastasia demanded something substantial for breakfast and Sabrina teased him about his coffee, he decided it didn't matter.

"I'm glad my two girls are feeling better," he said.

Anastasia had dressed in shorts and a T-shirt. Her shorter, wavy hair fluttered around her shoulders. It had only been a few weeks, but already she looked completely different from the malnourished waif they'd rescued.

"I feel great. Can we go in-line skating later? I think I'm getting better on the skates."

"You couldn't be getting worse," he teased.

Anastasia rolled her eyes. "Da-ad. I'm pretty good. Sabrina said so. And there are these two cute guys who always—"

Cal held up his hand. "You are twelve years old and you're not allowed to notice cute guys. Not until you're thirty. Understand?"

Sabrina chuckled. "Ignore him, kid. All fathers are like this. You're just gonna have to learn to deal with it."

Anastasia apparently chose to take her advice. "So can we, Dad?"

"Skating, yes. Guy noticing, no. How many pancakes?"

"Three for starters."

He turned his attention to Sabrina. She'd also showered and changed. Her shorts and T-shirt were similar to his daughter's, but his reaction to them was very different. While he thought Anastasia looked cute and stylish for a young girl, he thought Sabrina was about the sexiest creature he'd ever seen. Despite the mundane activity of preparing breakfast, he wanted her as much as he had before they'd made love.

"And you, young lady?"

"I'll start with a couple," she said, and touched her hand to her stomach. "I want to make sure I'm completely healed before I go showing off."

He wanted to be with her. On the beach, under the stars. He wanted—

"Let's go to Hawaii," he said without thinking.

Both females turned to look at him.

Cal shrugged. "Why not? It would be a real vacation. We'll get a bungalow on one of the islands." He looked at Anastasia. "You could learn to surf, we can go sailing. The weather is perfect. What do you say?"

"Oh, Dad, can we?"

"Sure." He turned to Sabrina. "You're quiet."

Her expression was unreadable and that made him nervous. "Cal, if you and Anastasia want to go, I think it's a great idea, but I'm afraid I can't join you."

He stared at her. What the hell was she talking about? "What do you mean? Of course you can join us." Didn't she want to be with him the way he wanted to be with her?

"I can't. I'm leaving." She looked away, but not before he caught the flash of guilt in her eyes. "It's just for a couple of days, but—"

"Leaving? You mean you want time off?" He knew he sounded stupid, but he couldn't help it. She'd never left before. If she wanted to visit her family, she did it while he was out of town. Did she want to get away from him?

"I have plenty of vacation time available," she snapped. "I'm taking a few days off. It's no big deal. I work for you, Cal, but you don't own me."

With that she stalked out of the room. Cal stared after her. He felt as if he'd been broadsided by a train. What had gone wrong?

"Daddy?" His daughter sounded shaken.

He gave her a quick hug. "I know, sweetie, but don't worry. I'll find out what's going on."

"You can fix it, can't you? You won't let Sabrina go away."

"I'll do the best I can." He kissed her head and wondered if he was about to let his daughter down.

Fourteen

Sabrina crossed to the window in her room and figured she had about thirty seconds of privacy before Cal came barging in to demand an explanation. She supposed she could have handled the situation worse, although right now it was hard to imagine that. Why had she reacted so badly? Why hadn't she said, in a calm voice, that she was thinking of visiting her family, or any other of a dozen acceptable excuses. Instead, she'd gotten angry and reminded him that he didn't own her. Dear Lord, had she really said that?

The answer to that and several other difficult questions was about three feet behind her. She'd gone to the trouble to make the bed, but the act of smoothing the covers and making sure the bedspread was centered didn't do much to erase the memories of the night they'd spent together. She wasn't stupid, so it didn't take her long to figure out that she'd reacted so badly because she was still reeling from the impact of their lovemaking. For Cal it had been…she shook her head. She didn't know what it had been to him. But for her, it had been a life-changing event. She knew that whatever happened, she would never love another man, or make love with another man, the way she'd loved and made love with him.

Talk about a sobering experience. Her life had been

completely turned around, and for all she knew, he'd simply scratched an itch.

It had been more wonderful than she'd thought it could ever be. She hugged her arms to her chest and rested her forehead against the cool glass of the window. Even now, when her body was pleasantly sore from all that they'd done together, she still wanted him. In her heart, she knew that she would always want him. That same organ informed her that he would never feel the same way about her. Sometimes the truth was ugly, but that didn't make it any less valid.

"Sabrina?"

She hadn't heard him enter the room, and it took a conscious effort not to flinch when he spoke. His voice rippled over her like warm water.

"I shouldn't have blurted it out like that," she said. "I don't mean to be difficult, but the truth is, I do have a lot of vacation time and I would like to take off for a few days."

"This isn't about you needing time away, is it? It's about last night."

She sucked in a breath. Dear Lord, give her the courage... The half-formed prayer trailed off. No, she wasn't about to pray that she lied well. She was going to have to figure out how to do that all on her own.

She opened her eyes and turned to face him. It was worse and more difficult than she'd imagined. He looked so perfect this morning, all freshly showered and so damn masculine. She wanted to weep. Now that she knew the truth, it was going to be harder than ever to walk away. Now that she'd felt his strength, and his gentleness, now that she'd tasted him, had him taste her, now that she'd experienced the passion and the need and the magic. She didn't think she had the strength to leave. But she knew she didn't have the strength to stay and watch him grow tired of her, then turn his attention on someone else. She could suffer deeply and quickly, then get over it, or she could die a little each day.

It wasn't much of a choice.

"I was going to tell you later," she said. "Last night has nothing to do with it. I do need some time off. But not to visit my family."

He frowned. "You need to get away from me?"

She smiled. "Amazingly enough, Cal, this isn't about you at all. I got a phone call yesterday morning. Do you remember?"

He nodded.

"It was from someone in New York. A headhunter. He's set up a few interviews for me. That's where I'm going. To New York. I'm leaving the company."

Until she said the words, she hadn't been sure she was really going to go through with it. But as soon as she spoke, she knew she'd made the right decision. It would be so easy to stay and love Cal forever, to make the decision to die day by day until there was nothing left but an empty shell where a heart and soul had once lived. This was harder, but ultimately better.

Which didn't explain why she felt as if she were bleeding to death.

She'd thought about this moment a hundred times. She figured Anastasia would express sorrow, but Cal would just take it in stride. She'd pictured the moment, the quiet raising of one eyebrow, the faint smile. "I hate to see you go, but you have to do what's right. Are you sure there's nothing I can do to make you stay?" He would be disappointed, maybe even a bit uneasy about breaking in a new assistant—but he wouldn't be devastated. She'd schooled herself to accept *his* acceptance with equal, casual grace.

She hadn't expected the color to drain from his face or his expression to freeze. She hadn't expected him to glare at her accusingly. "You're leaving?"

His question put her on the defensive. "It was bound to happen. You can't have expected me to work for you forever."

He shoved his hands into his pockets and stared at her. His silence made her uneasy.

"It's not that I don't like my job," she said. "I do. I love the travel and the challenge. You're great to work for. But I need more. I need—"

"What? What do you need? Explain it to me."

She shrugged. "I don't know how to put it into words." Actually she did, but what made sense in her head had the chance of sounding stupid in real life. "The work is demanding." She held up a hand to keep him from interrupting. "I don't mind that. In fact I like it a lot. But I don't have any time left over for a personal life."

"You have days off. Evenings, too."

"When you travel, I go with you. When you want to work late, I'm there at the office. The only time I get to be on my own is when you're out on a date. If you're between women, we're together constantly. That has made it impossible for me to make friends and see them."

"You mean a man."

"I mean friends. My whole life revolves around you, Cal. I haven't minded. In fact, I still don't mind, but I need more."

"I see." But his tone told her he didn't see at all.

Sabrina was confused. If she didn't know better, she

would say that Cal was hurt by what she was telling him. That didn't make sense. She'd hoped he would miss her, but this silent accusing reaction was unexpected.

"I've really enjoyed working for you. I've learned a lot, but it's time to move on."

"So you're leaving." It wasn't a question.

"Yes."

"And last night? That wasn't an attempt at a relationship, was it? You were interested in stud service."

She winced. "Cal, it wasn't like that."

He took a step toward her, then stopped. Fire flared in his eyes, but this time it came from anger and hurt, not passion. "It sure the hell wasn't for me. I don't know what you were thinking, though. 'Hey, I'm outta here so let's screw the boss once, just so I can say I did.' Is that it?"

"No, never. I wanted—" She pressed her lips together. She didn't know what to say. In an odd twist of events she didn't completely understand, *she* was the one on the defensive. She was pretty sure the nagging feeling at the back of her mind was guilt.

"I haven't done anything wrong," she said hotly. "I refuse to feel bad about what happened. You wanted it, too."

"Yes, I did." He stared at her. "Why, Sabrina? Why did you want to make love with me?"

She couldn't answer that one. The truth would only make things worse. He wouldn't want to hear it and she couldn't stand the humiliation. "What was last night to you?" she asked, hoping to shift the focus of the conversation.

His mouth twisted at the corner. "Very special. Something I'll treasure always."

That hit her where she lived. She felt her eyes burn and had to fight tears. "I refuse to feel guilty about leaving," she whispered. "I have every right to go."

"Yes, you do."

"I worked hard for you. I gave you everything I had. I was worth every penny."

"That was never in question."

The tears came, anyway. She felt them roll down her cheeks and had to brush them away. What had gone wrong? When had she lost control of the conversation?

"I'll be gone only a few days," she said. "When I get back, I'll start looking for a replacement." She sucked in a breath. "As of now, I'm giving you thirty days' notice that I'm quitting."

Cal flinched slightly and headed for the door. She wanted him to yell at her and refuse to let her go. She wanted him to throw her on the bed and make love with her until she changed her mind. She wanted him to tell her that she would never be happy with anyone but him. She wanted him to say that he loved her.

He said nothing.

When he reached the doorway, he turned back to face her. This time she was sure she saw pain in his eyes and in the lines bracketing his mouth. But she was confused and didn't know what it meant.

"I don't want a replacement, Sabrina. I've only ever wanted you," he said, then left.

She stared after him, knowing that he was talking about work and desperately wishing he meant something else.

As Cal headed downstairs, he tried to think. Sabrina couldn't be leaving. It wasn't right. She'd been a part of his life for so long, he wasn't sure he could survive without her. This wasn't just about business, either, although he would miss her presence in that area, too. But mostly this was personal. He'd come to depend upon her. He cared about her and had believed she cared about him. How could she walk away from all that?

He crossed to the patio and stared out at the ocean. She was leaving to have a life. What was wrong with the one she had here...with him? Why did she need someone else? He knew that's what she was talking about. Dating, falling in love, maybe even getting married.

He frowned, trying to remember if Sabrina ever dated. He recalled her mentioning a couple of guys, but that had been a while ago. There hadn't been anyone special in the past couple of years. He'd had a series of women, but she'd been alone.

He didn't like it, but in a way he could understand it. Sabrina was a lovely, vital, giving woman. She needed more. If only—

"Daddy?"

He turned as Anastasia rushed at him. There were tears in her eyes. He held out his arms and she ran into his embrace.

"Daddy, don't let Sabrina leave. I don't want her to go."

He hugged his daughter close. "I don't want her to go, either, sweetie, but we don't get a choice in this one."

"No!" A sob shook her.

"I know it's hard to understand, but Sabrina has her own life. She only works for me, and that means she's free to leave whenever she wants."

Anastasia clung to him. "She's going forever?"

"Right now she's leaving for a few days. Then she'll be back."

He figured there was no point in dumping the rest of it on his daughter. The time would come when he would have to explain that Sabrina had given notice. But he wanted Anastasia to get used to this smaller hurt, first.

He rocked her in his arms. When the crying slowed, he suggested a board game to distract them both. They'd been playing for about an hour when Sabrina walked out onto the patio. She'd showered and changed. Instead of casual shorts and a T-shirt, she wore tailored slacks and a silk blouse. She had a jacket slung over one arm.

"I made some phone calls," she said. "I have a flight to New York later this morning. The shuttle will be here in a few minutes."

It hurt to look at her. Cal didn't want to think about how bad it was going to be when she was gone. "You don't even want me to drive you to the airport?"

She flinched. "It wasn't that." She motioned to the game. "I didn't want to disrupt your game."

"I see." But he knew the truth. She didn't want to spend any more time with him than she had to. "How long will you be gone?"

"A few days. Maybe a week. I'll be in touch."

He shrugged, as if it didn't matter. Inside, though, he could feel a sharp pain building. He had a feeling it would never go away. "Don't worry about us. We'll be fine."

Sabrina nodded. She bit her lower lip. "I'll miss you, Anastasia."

The girl turned toward the view. Cal saw her wipe away a tear, but her voice was strong and uncaring as she said, "I won't miss you, Sabrina. You're just the hired help. I'm sure my father will find someone to replace you."

Sabrina winced. "I'm sure he will." She turned to Cal. "I'm really sorry about all of this."

Anastasia's chair scraped against the cement patio as she pushed it back and lunged for Sabrina. Tears streamed down her face.

"Don't go," the girl sobbed. "Don't go away. I'll miss you so much. I didn't mean that. I will miss you."

Sabrina pulled her close. "I know, honey. I'll miss you, too."

"Then why are you leaving?"

"Good question," Cal told her.

Sabrina stared at him. "I have to."

Anastasia stepped back and wiped her face with the back of her hand. "Is my dad leaving next? Are you all leaving me?"

Fresh tears rolled down her cheeks. Cal rose and moved next to her. "I'm not leaving you, Anastasia. You're my daughter and you're going to be with me forever."

The preteen shook her head. "No. Everybody leaves me."

Sabrina touched her hair. "It's not like that."

"Yes, it is."

Cal hugged her. "No, it's not. I have a lot of flaws, kid, but I always keep my word. You can ask Sabrina. I promise I won't leave you, Anastasia. No matter what, I'll be here for you."

"Sabrina?"

Sabrina gave her a shaky smile. "He's right. He does keep his word. You can trust him."

Cal felt his daughter's thin arms wrap around him.

She shook as she cried. Over her head, he met Sabrina's gaze. He wanted to ask why she was doing this to them. Where else was she needed as much? But he couldn't speak. The words got stuck in his throat, and by the time they were loose, the shuttle driver had knocked on the front door.

"Cal, I—"

"No, Sabrina. It's what you want. Just go."

She left without saying goodbye. He told himself they would all be fine. That time was a great healer. But as he held his devastated daughter and felt his own heart slowly crumbling, he wasn't sure he believed it was ever going to be true.

That night, Cal lay stretched out on top of his daughter's bed. Anastasia was next to him, curled close under the covers. He turned the page in the book and kept reading. When he reached the end of the chapter, she glanced up at him.

"I'm way too old for this," she pointed out.

"I'm reading to you because we both like it, not because of your age. It's fun."

"I know, but it makes me feel like a kid."

"I hate to point this out, but you are a kid."

"Na-uh."

"Uh-huh." He touched the tip of her nose. "You're my kid."

She leaned her head against his arm. "She's not going to call tonight, is she?"

He knew the "she" in question was Sabrina. He glanced at the clock. It was nearly ten. Her flight had taken off around eleven that morning, which put her into New York about eight, East Coast time. She would have reached the hotel by ten, which was only seven, their time.

"No," he said quietly. "She's not going to call."

He wanted to protest the unfairness of it all. When he'd gone away, *he'd* called. She should have the common courtesy to do the same. But there was no one to complain to.

"I miss her," Anastasia said.

"Me, too."

"But we're gonna be okay without her, aren't we? I mean, we're fine on our own."

Her need for reassurance was painfully obvious. He kissed the top of her head. "We're better than fine. We're perfect in every way."

His daughter giggled. "Da-ad."

"It's true. You and I are doing great. We had a rocky start, but we've recovered. We're getting to know each other. The whole parent-child relationship can be difficult for both sides, and we're going to have things to work through, but I'm not worried. You're a good kid."

She smiled. "You're a good dad."

Her brown eyes were similar to his. He'd often searched her features, trying to figure out what came from him and what she'd inherited from Janice. In many ways, Anastasia was her own person. Perhaps he recognized that more easily than most parents because he'd only recently met her. He hadn't had a part of her early years.

"I'm sorry I didn't know about you before," he said. "I would have liked to have been there from the beginning."

"Really?"

He nodded. "You're very special."

He felt that tightening in his chest again and recognized it for what it was. Love. He, who had grown up in a cold, unwelcoming home, had finally learned how to love someone.

"I love you, Anastasia. No matter what, I'll always love you." As he spoke the words, he felt a great warmth inside.

She buried her head against his chest. "I love you, too, Daddy," she whispered.

He closed his eyes to savor the moment, to try to make it enough, but it wasn't. No matter how much he loved his daughter, he still missed Sabrina. How had he let her go? How was he going to survive without her around? What choice did he have but to figure it out? As much as he wanted to, he couldn't *make* her stay.

Anastasia read his mind. "What about Sabrina, Daddy? She needs to be with us."

"I know it feels that way now, but we'll get used to having her gone."

"I don't think so."

"We don't have a choice. We can't force her to stay. She wants her own life. She likes her job, but it's just that. A job. She's not family, like you and me."

His daughter drew her knees up to her chest and smoothed the covers. "If you married her, she'd be a part of the family and she'd stay. Married people live together."

She imparted the last tidbit in the tone of someone sharing a seldom-discussed fact.

Cal opened his mouth, then closed it. Marry Sabrina? *Marry* Sabrina? "I can't," he said without thinking.

"Why not? You like her, I know you do. If you get married, she'll have to stay. We'll be her life."

218 LONE STAR MILLIONAIRE

Cal felt as if he were tumbling through space. It wasn't that the thought of marrying Sabrina was so horrible. The idea stunned him, but he had a feeling he could get used to it. The difficulty lay in the asking.

"It's not that simple."

Anastasia rolled her eyes. "Adults make everything so complicated."

"That's true."

Later, when she was finally asleep, he walked out onto the beach and stared at the waves. In the darkness they were vague shapes topped by white foam. He inhaled the scent of salt, sand and sea. For the rest of his life, when he thought of Sabrina, this is the smell he would remember. This and the sweetness that was her body.

Marry her, Anastasia had said. It would solve all their problems. Cal was willing to admit that, in theory, that was true. It sounded so simple. Just ask her. Be with her. Love her.

He closed his eyes. Loving Anastasia was safe. She was his child and that bonded them together. But Sabrina was different. She was a woman, at times a difficult and challenging woman. He admired her and respected her and wanted her. But love her? Did he dare?

It would be too easy to let himself fall for her. Maybe he already had. And then what? She could never love him back. That was what he couldn't explain to his daughter. Sabrina knew the worst about him. She'd seen into the darkness of his soul. She liked him. Apparently she even wanted him in her bed. But love? She was too good. She would choose a very different kind of man.

The truth was, Anastasia was the first person to ever love him. His parents hadn't, his sister had been too self-absorbed. The women who came and went in his life saw him as a means to an end. He didn't try to fool himself about that. Even Janice hadn't wanted to be with him longer than she had to. She'd gotten herself pregnant but had been careful to ensure they didn't have to marry.

Sabrina was worth ten of Janice. She was an amazing woman. And she'd seen him with Tiffany and Colette and all the others. She knew how he operated. She would never trust him. She would never love him back.

The kindest act would be to let her go.

Sabrina had indulged herself with a first-class airline ticket. Traveling with Cal had spoiled her, probably for good. The flight attendant offered her wine, but she refused. She had too much thinking to do and she needed a clear head.

The time in New York had gone by quickly. She'd had two job offers in the past five days. One with a firm in New York, the other with a company based out of Chicago. The jobs were equally fabulous with great pay and benefits and lots of room for advancement. It was as if each company had read her wish list and decided to make her dreams come true. All she had to do was decide.

So in this moment, when she should be celebrating and planning her future, why was she so sad? Why did she keep thinking about Cal and Anastasia and wondering what they were doing? Why was she still hurt because they hadn't been home when she'd called to tell them she was on her way back? She'd left a message with the information on the answering machine, but it wasn't the same. She'd wanted to talk to them. She desperately wanted to hear Cal's voice.

Loving him and leaving him was going to be harder than she'd first imagined. Life without him would be empty and cold for a long time. Logically she knew she wasn't going to die of a broken heart, even if it felt like it right now. And the worst wasn't over. She didn't just have to tell Cal about the job offers, she had to go through the trauma of hiring someone else.

There would be interviews, then making a final choice. Worst of all, she would then lie awake at night and picture that other person living her life, taking care of Cal the way she had. She wasn't sure how she would get over that.

If only she'd never fallen in love with him. Sabrina clutched the arms of the seat. Loving him was something she did very well. She couldn't regret that. In the deepest, darkest part of her she knew she would rather have loved him and miss him when she left, than be with someone else. Which made her a lovesick fool.

She reached for the headsets and put them on. With a little luck someone had written a country music song about her sorry life and she could find out how it was all going to come out in the end.

Fifteen

Sabrina collected her carry-on suitcase and headed for the door. She hadn't bothered to arrange a shuttle for her return trip, so she was going to have to call the company when she retrieved the rest of her luggage. Or maybe she could take a cab. She followed the other first-class passengers down the jet way. There was the usual crowd of people, family members and friends to greet those arriving. She didn't bother to check for any familiar faces.

She'd already started toward baggage claim area when she heard someone calling her name.

"Sabrina! We're over here."

She turned and saw Cal with Anastasia. The girl was grinning and waving madly. Cal's expression was more difficult to read, but there was a light in his dark eyes that made her hope he was pleased to see her.

"We missed you," Anastasia said, rushing toward her and giving her a hug. "We've had lots of fun doing stuff, but we missed you."

Sabrina brushed the girl's hair off her forehead. "I missed you, too." She looked up at her boss and gave him a shy smile. "Thanks for picking me up, Cal. I appreciate it."

"I know it's not fun to come home alone." He had a hand tucked behind his back, and when he drew it around in front of him, she saw he held a single red rose. "For you," he said. "Anastasia's right. We missed you very much."

She took the flower, brought it to her nose and inhaled the scent. The actions kept her distracted enough to allow her to blink back the tears that formed. The last time they'd seen each other, they'd come as close to fighting as they ever had in all the years she'd known him. She was three weeks away from walking out of his life forever. So why was he being so nice to her?

"Let's go get your luggage," he said as he put one arm around his daughter and the other around her. "So tell me about your trip. Was it successful?"

"Define *success*."

"Did you get any job offers?"

"Two." She mentioned the names of the companies. As they went down the escalator to the baggage claim area, then waited for the luggage, she talked about her interviews.

"They're both good companies," he said. "I don't know how you're going to like winters in either New York or Chicago, but you'll survive."

"I know." His touch was sure and familiar. She wanted to burrow closer to him and ask him to promise to always be there. What a mistake. So Cal had missed her. It didn't mean anything significant. He was probably regretting the fact that he'd had to do all the cooking. No doubt he wasn't looking forward to breaking in a new assistant. After all, they'd been together six years. For him it was an inconvenience, but for her, it was going to be major heartbreak. Still, she knew it was the right thing to do.

Anastasia stepped close and lowered her voice. "I met a boy," she said shyly.

Cal winced. "You did not meet a boy. I won't allow

that. She went in-line skating with some kids her age. Children of both sexes. There will be no boy-meeting until you're thirty. Maybe not even then!''

Anastasia giggled. ''His name is Jason and he's really cute.''

''Cute is not allowed,'' Cal informed her. ''I told you that already. No cute, no boys, none of that.''

Sabrina grinned. ''What's he like?''

When Cal would have started in on her, too, she pointed to the moving carousel. ''That's my suitcase,'' she said. ''The navy one.''

He grunted, then went to pick it up.

''He's nice,'' Anastasia said in a low voice. ''He's a year older than me and he's really great on blades. When I went skating with everyone, he showed me a couple of turns and stuff. I'm getting a lot better. There's a group of us going skating again tomorrow. Can you talk to Dad so he'll let me go?''

''I don't want to get caught in the middle,'' Sabrina started to say. At Anastasia's look of disappointment, she sighed. ''Okay, I'll see what I can do.''

''Thanks.''

Cal returned carrying the suitcase. ''What is she thanking you for? What have you agreed to do?''

Sabrina took his arm and led him toward the short-term parking. ''Nothing you have to worry yourself about. Everything is going to be fine.''

''You think I don't know when you're lying to me?'' He gave her a mock glare. ''Is this another of those 'he's male so he must be stupid' things? I'm not stupid.''

Sabrina glanced at his daughter. ''Wow, when did he get so sensitive about stuff?''

"I don't know. I guess it's because he's only around women."

"You're right," Sabrina said. "He needs some testosterone. Maybe he can get a shot or take vitamins."

"Like I need this," Cal muttered.

He caught her eye and grinned. She smiled back. It felt so right to be with him, she thought. She didn't know how much he'd really missed her, but she was willing to bet she'd missed him about ten times as much.

After unlocking the trunk, Cal handed his daughter the keys. She opened the car and scrambled into the back seat. Cal put the suitcase into the trunk and closed it. He turned to Sabrina.

"You deliberately stayed away from oil and gas companies, didn't you?"

She nodded. "I didn't want to create any illusion of conflict of interest."

"I'm not going to make you sign anything. If you'd rather stay in the industry, I wouldn't mind."

She looked at him. When high-placed employees left a firm in any industry, it was standard practice to have them sign a clause stating they wouldn't steal customers, compete directly or go to work for a competitor for a specified period of time. She'd just assumed Cal would want her to sign one.

"Why not?" she asked.

"You'll get a better job if you stay where you already have expertise. I want you to do well."

It was all she could do not to fling herself at him. "You're a really nice guy," she said.

"I know, but keep it to yourself. I have a reputation I have to keep intact."

"I won't breathe a word."

He walked around to her side of the car and held the door open. His hand rested on top of the window. She placed hers on his. "Thanks, Cal. I won't do anything to hurt the company."

"I know. That's why I offered."

"I'm going to find you the best replacement. You won't even notice I'm gone."

He didn't say anything for a couple of seconds, then he smiled. But it didn't reach his eyes, and she had the feeling it was more for show than because he was happy. "Let's not talk about that," he said. "Right now I just want to enjoy having you here."

Later that night Sabrina stood at the front of the porch and leaned toward the ocean. "I had a view of Central Park from my hotel room," she said. "It was nice, but nothing like this."

She heard Cal move up behind her, then he wrapped his arms around her waist. She hadn't realized how much she'd missed being close to him until that minute. Her body fit perfectly against his. He was warm and strong, and Lord help her, she wanted him.

"People say that folks from Texas talk funny, but if you ask me, those New York Yankees can be mighty tough to understand," he said, broadening his accent.

"I agree. Life is different there." She placed her hands on top of his. "Life is different here, too. More relaxed. I like it." She took a deep breath. "I'm sorry about Hawaii, not being able to go, I mean."

"It's all right. I was trying to extend the fantasy." His voice rumbled against her back. "Reality isn't so bad. I haven't forgotten what it was like, Sabrina. What we were like when we were together."

He rested his chin on her shoulder. She instinctively

tilted her head, exposing her neck. He turned toward her and brushed his lips against her skin. A shiver rippled down her spine.

"I don't know that I've ever really missed anyone before," he said quietly. "But I missed you. I thought about you constantly while you were gone."

His confession touched her, making her want to confess all to him. That she'd missed him, too. That she wanted him, that she loved him and had probably loved him from the first.

"Between you and Anastasia, I think you're making a difference in me," he said. "I'm still something of a jerk, but I'm getting better."

She closed her eyes. "I never thought you were a jerk, Cal. I've always admired you."

"I'm glad. Your good opinion matters to me. I would do almost anything to keep it, but there are some things I just can't resist."

His hold on her loosened, and as he released her, he turned her toward him. She knew he was going to kiss her and she met him halfway, her mouth already parted and ready for him.

This wasn't like before. There was no playfulness, no teasing, little conversation. Last time they'd been caught up in exploration, this time they were drowning in need. The fire erupted instantly, surrounding them with passionate flames.

He held her face in his hands as he kissed her. His mouth was open, his tongue sought hers. Over and over he stroked and circled, danced and caressed.

"I want you," he murmured. "I want you in my bed. Naked. On your back, hungry for me. Wet and ready. I want to be in you, filling you, making you mine."

His words stunned her. When he broke the kiss and took her hand to lead her up the stairs, she followed mindlessly. If he'd sought to paint a verbal picture of them making love, he'd succeeded. She couldn't imagine being anywhere else or *with* anyone else.

They reached his room. Lights from the street filtered in through the vertical blinds. He didn't bother turning on any of the lamps. In the semidarkness, they reached for each other, hands touching, clothing falling, until at last they were naked.

He drew her onto the bed. She went willingly, wanting him to do all the things he'd talked about, wanting to feel those things with him. Only with him.

He kissed her passionately. As the world began to spin, he was her only constant and she had to cling to him to maintain her place in the universe. His muscles were warm and rippling beneath her hands. She moved up and down his back, rediscovering the familiar country that was his body. He, too, familiarized himself with her. He started at her collarbone and moved lower. When he reached her breasts, he cupped one yielding curve, learning its shape and weight. Her nipple tightened. He toyed with the taut tip, rubbing it with the pad of his thumb, circling around, sending waves of wanting through her.

He deepened the kiss. She closed her lips over his tongue and sucked gently. He groaned low in his throat. His arousal bumped against her thigh. She moved a hand down between them and encircled the length of him. His skin there was so soft, like shorn velvet, but inside he was hard as steel. She liked the shape of him, the definition, the vein running down the back, the way he flexed when she stroked him.

A single drop of moisture lay on the very tip. She

used her forefinger to smooth it over him. The dampness made him slick and reminded her of what it would be like when he was inside her.

As if he read her mind, he moved his hand lower, over her belly, past the protective curls to that secret place between her thighs. She parted for him, wanting him there. His fingers were sure as they moved down into the moist heat. He caressed either side of the most sensitive part of her before dipping inside and mimicking the act of love.

Fingers moved in and out, preparing her until she felt she couldn't possibly be more swollen or wet. She moved her hand faster, urging him onward. He broke the kiss long enough to kneel between her legs and put on protection, then he slid home.

Within two thrusts she was on the edge of discovery. By the third, the familiar pressure began and she found herself spiraling out of control. But this was different from before. The release brought its own tension, and she knew she had entered a new dimension of pleasure.

He braced himself above her, eyes open, studying her. She clutched at him and urged him deeper. Love filled her, along with the desire. It was a heady combination.

A few more thrusts and another climax. She felt him nearing his release and her tension grew again. She tried to hold back, to contain herself.

"Don't," he ground out. "Don't resist. Give in. Come for me, Sabrina. Now!"

His words freed her. She exploded, deeply and completely, giving herself over to the spasms. He plunged into her one last time and groaned his own contentment. She felt herself milking him dry.

When they had caught their breath, they clung to

each other. There was much to talk about, Sabrina thought, but she didn't have the words. Whatever happened, she would always be able to remember this night. She suspected no man would ever come close to touching her as completely as Cal. There might be other lovers, other good times, but he had possession of her heart. Perhaps she should try to reclaim it, if such a thing were possible. But in an odd way, she wanted him to keep it with him always.

She loved him, and right now, in his arms, with the scent of their lovemaking clinging to them both, it was enough.

The tinkle of glass followed by a muttered swear word woke her the next morning. Sabrina raised her head and saw Cal standing in the doorway to his bedroom, tray in hand.

"Sorry," he said when he saw she was awake. "I wanted to surprise you with breakfast. I know it's early, but I'd hoped we could have some time together before Anastasia woke up."

The combination of the thoughtful gesture, not to mention the little-boy smile, made him impossible to resist. She pulled the sheet up so it covered her breasts, then sat against the headboard.

"You're very sweet. Is there coffee, too?"

"What's breakfast without coffee?"

She glanced with interest at the tray. "And I wasn't sure you even knew how to work a toaster. I'll reserve judgment until I taste everything."

He set the tray next to her. "I'm crushed you don't trust me."

He'd dressed in shorts and a T-shirt, but he hadn't showered or shaved yet. Stubble darkened his jaw and his hair was mussed. She'd seen him in a perfectly tailored suit, even a tuxedo, but to her, he'd never looked more handsome...or appealing.

"Thank you," she said, and reached for the mug. "You are a prince without equal."

"No, but I am one of the world's most eligible bachelors."

She chuckled. "I'd forgotten about that. Getting any fan mail yet?"

But if he answered, she didn't hear. Sabrina wasn't sure of anything at that moment. Her gaze fell on the small white velvet box sitting in the center of the tray. The coffee mug had shadowed it, which was why she hadn't noticed it before.

She put the mug on the nightstand so she wouldn't drop it. Her stomach knotted until the pain was nearly unbearable. She knew her heart still had to be beating, but she couldn't feel it. She couldn't feel anything but the agony of knowing that it was over before it had begun.

He'd come to her last night knowing he was going to do this today. The betrayal nearly made her gag. It was too early for him to have gone out to get the parting gift this morning. He'd planned ahead. Damn him. And damn her for believing in him. She *knew* better.

"Sabrina?" Cal sat down next to her. "What's wrong?"

He was going to tell her goodbye while she was naked. She wasn't sure why that particular thought stuck in her head, but it did. Naked and vulnerable and there wasn't anything she could do about it.

"Sabrina?"

She cleared her throat. "It's too small for a watch.

Too bad, because we both know I can tell time the old-fashioned way.''

Her voice sounded almost normal. If someone didn't know her really well, he wouldn't have been able to guess. Unfortunately, Cal did know her.

"A watch? What are you talking about? Tell me what's wrong."

She pointed to the jeweler's box, not daring to touch it. "That. The 'it's over' gift. How thoughtful of you to choose it yourself. Or did Anastasia help?''

"No!" He took her hands in his. "I'm sorry. I'm doing this all wrong, aren't I? I wanted to surprise you. I thought this would be romantic. I forgot about those stupid gifts I sent women when it was over." He stared at her intently. "You have to believe me. This isn't like that."

He released her long enough to pick up the small velvet box and open it. She forced herself to be strong and look inside.

Instead of a pin or a pair of earrings, a beautiful emerald-cut diamond solitaire winked back at her. She blinked. "I don't understand. You never give rings."

One corner of his mouth turned up. "I'm not telling you it's over. I'm trying to propose. Sabrina, I want you to marry me."

There was a rushing in her ears. She glanced from him to the ring and back. His smile broadened. "You're proposing?"

"Yes. Marry me. Please."

With the possible exception of telling her he'd had regression therapy and had remembered a past life as a dog, she couldn't think of anything he could have said that would have shocked her more. Marry him? Calhoun Jefferson Langtry was proposing to *her?*

The rushing in her ears turned to a ringing, and her stomach stopped hurting, but now it was flopping around. She felt light-headed and confused. Why did he want to marry her?

She searched his face, hoping to find a clue. She knew him well enough to know that he wouldn't have asked lightly. Nor would he change his mind and retract the proposal. Did he care about her the way she cared about him? He hadn't said anything about love, but obviously...

Then she knew. The ringing stopped, her stomach settled down to normal. She closed the velvet box.

"You don't want to lose me," she said flatly.

"Of course not." He touched her cheek. "You're a part of my life."

"You're right. We're good friends, we work well together. We get along. We're well matched, personality-wise and in bed. I keep your life running smoothly and I've already established a relationship with your daughter."

He frowned. "I want to agree with everything you've said, but I sense a trap."

"No trap, Cal. Just the truth." It hurt to breathe. She felt as if her heart had collapsed on itself. She'd come so close to realizing her dream. She hadn't known how much she'd allowed herself to hope until it was all snatched away from her.

"If I wanted to keep my job, would that be a problem?" she asked.

"No. Do you want to?"

She ignored his question. "Stock options? Are they available?"

The frown deepened. "You're making this sound like a business transaction. It's not like that. I want to marry you, Sabrina. I want a relationship. I will try to be a good husband.''

She nodded. "I know you, and you *will* try. You'll be faithful and caring." He would drive her to the limits of pleasure in bed, too, if she let him.

It was so tempting. They could have children together. She would never have to worry about money. Of course she was already fairly well off now. But there would be security, and respect. Many marriages had survived on less.

But he didn't love her. He didn't love anyone, except maybe his daughter. She knew herself well enough to know that a loveless marriage would destroy her. After a while she would dry up and blow away. What was the saying? Ashes to ashes, dust to dust.

She loved him, therefore she couldn't marry him.

She climbed out of bed and slipped on her clothes, then crossed to the door. "I'm sorry, Cal," she said. "I...I can't."

Sixteen

Cal wasn't sure how long he sat alone in the kitchen. It could have been ten minutes or two hours. He couldn't think, he couldn't do anything but wait for the pain to ease a little. He'd tried. That's what he told himself. He'd done his best and he'd failed. At the time it had seemed so simple. That he would propose and she would say yes, and she would stay with him always. That's what he'd wanted, but it hadn't happened.

He supposed he couldn't blame her for refusing him. He didn't have anything to offer her. After all, she knew the worst about him. She'd been there all the times he'd gotten involved with silly, inappropriate women. Women he'd chosen because they were pretty and easy and they didn't challenge him in any way. Women he could walk away from without giving them a second's thought. He'd been so afraid of someone real. Someone he could love, someone like her.

He'd thought being alone was the worst thing in the world, but now he knew better. The worst thing in the world was being without her.

He heard a noise in the hallway and glanced up. His daughter stepped into the room. She walked over and hugged him. "'Morning, Daddy."

He held her close. "Good morning."

She stepped back and looked at him. "What's wrong?"

Apparently he was so transparent even his twelve-year-old kid knew something was troubling him. "Nothing."

"Da-ad."

"Don't 'Da-ad' me," he told her. "What do you want for breakfast?"

"Nothing. Did something happen with Sabrina?"

He couldn't tell her the truth. Not yet. She'd already been hurt by so much. He swore to himself. Not only was he going to have to figure out how to survive without the one woman he loved, but his daughter was also going to have to get used to living without her. It wasn't fair.

"Cereal or pancakes?" he asked, deliberately keeping his voice light.

Anastasia pushed her glasses higher onto her nose and sighed. "Cereal is fine. It's Sabrina, isn't it? Did you talk to her about staying?"

He got down a bowl. "Eat first, talk later."

Sabrina moved closer to the ocean. It was still early enough that she had most of the beach to herself. Which was good. She wasn't in the mood to smile at strangers, and she had a bad feeling that if someone asked even a simple question, like "How are you?" she would burst into tears.

What had gone wrong? Why had he proposed to her?

She shook her head. She knew the answer to that one. The problem was, she wanted it to be for a different reason. She wanted Cal to have asked her to marry him because he loved her and couldn't imagine living without her, not because she was a convenience. That made her feel like a dishwasher.

She shoved her hands into her jeans pockets and

sighed. The worse part was, she was tempted. The weakness invaded her, making her want to go to him and tell him that she would agree to marry him under any conditions. After all, he would be a good husband. He would be faithful to her. She knew he cared about her and respected her. Maybe, in time, he could fall in love with her. Wasn't that a possibility? Wasn't that enough? A good man, Anastasia, children of her own. Was she wishing for the moon to want more?

She bit her lower lip. She couldn't settle. Not on this issue. It wasn't right. And if she did, she would never be able to respect herself. Some of Cal wasn't better than none. She would make a clean break of it. Sure it would be difficult, but she would recover and go on. There were lots of men out there who would find her interesting. She might fall in love with one of them. If not, she could like one a lot and try to make a go of it.

Which was settling in a different way, she thought sadly. So what was the answer?

She walked for several more minutes before turning around and heading back to the house. One thing she knew for sure—she was going to tell Cal the truth. Before she actually left, she was going to gather her courage together and admit that she'd fallen in love with him and that was the reason she couldn't accept his proposal. She had enough to regret already; she wasn't going to spend her life wishing she'd told him how she felt. She smiled thinking of his confusion when she carefully explained that the reason she wouldn't marry him was because she loved him too much.

As she neared their rented place, her mind filled with memories. There had been so many good times over the past six years. So much laughter and teasing, so many wonderful moments. The party he'd thrown for her when she turned twenty-five. How he'd come with her when her youngest sister had graduated from college. The extra-long weekend in Hong Kong after she'd won their stock bet last year. The specialist he'd had flown in when they were afraid that Gram had suffered a heart attack. So many wonderful gestures, so much affection. Cal might not have loved her, but he'd been a good friend. Along with her confession of love, she was going to tell him that, too. He was a wonderful man. Now that he'd let his daughter into his heart, he needed to make room for someone else. Someone who would treasure him and take care of him.

Thinking about him with another woman hurt too much, so she pushed the thought away. She crossed the sand to the boardwalk, then stepped into their patio. The sliding glass door was open. Cal and Anastasia were in the kitchen. They didn't see her as she stepped into the living room.

The preteen put a bowl into the sink and turned to face her father. "Okay, I ate my breakfast. Now tell me what happened."

Sabrina stopped in her tracks. Anastasia knew about the proposal?

Cal shrugged. "There's nothing to tell." He held up his hand. "I'm not kidding. I asked her to marry me and she said no. That's it."

"That's not it. Start at the beginning and tell me everything. She couldn't have said no. She loves you, Daddy, I know she does."

Even if Sabrina had wanted to leave, the girl's words rooted her in place. She shifted until she was concealed by the bookcase against the dividing wall and sucked in her breath. How had Anastasia figured out the truth?

"I wish that were true," Cal said. "But it's not. Sweetie, I know you wanted this to work out, and I did, too. Sometimes grown-ups make life complicated."

"What does that have to do with anything?"

"Sabrina and I have known each other for a long time."

"I know. You get along great. She wants to marry you. You must have said something to make her mad."

If she hadn't been so frozen with shock, she might have smiled at the preteen's assumption.

"I did not." Cal sounded indignant. "I took her breakfast in bed. There was an engagement ring in a velvet box on the tray. I asked her to marry me and she said no. End of story."

Sabrina heard a rustling sound, then Anastasia spoke, but her voice was muffled. "I'm sorry, Daddy. I really thought she loved you. I don't understand."

She risked a glance and saw Cal hugging his daughter.

"I've seen how she looks at you," the girl continued. "It's exactly how my mom looked at my other dad. You look at her the same way. I hate this. I don't ever want to grow up."

"Sorry, kid, you don't get a choice." He drew in a deep breath. "Don't blame Sabrina, okay? It's not her fault."

"Yes, it is!"

"No. I'm the one who..."

When he paused, Sabrina risked another glance. Cal stood with his back to her. He rested his chin on his daughter's head.

"I'm the one who messed up. See, Sabrina knows me too well. We all have bad parts, and usually we keep them hidden from the world. The problem is, Sabrina has seen those parts of me. They're pretty awful and she can't forget that. She's so wonderful. Bright. Funny. Pretty. She can do a lot better than me."

"No way," his daughter said loyally.

"Thanks, but on this one, you're wrong. Any guy would be lucky to have her."

Sabrina pressed her fingers to her mouth to keep from crying out. She knew the man, recognized his appearance and the sound of his voice, but she couldn't believe what he was saying. She'd never heard him talk like this before. What did it mean?

A gladness filled her heart. She didn't want to risk hoping and having those hopes dashed, but she couldn't control the feeling that grew and grew until it burned hot and bright like the sun.

"Daddy, if you love someone, you love all the parts inside. Sometimes I can be, you know, sorta bratty, but you love me."

"It's more than just sorta bratty, and yes, I do love you, but that's different."

"Why? You love Sabrina."

"Yes, but she doesn't love me."

Her legs nearly gave way. Yes. He'd said yes. As in yes, he loved her!

"What did she say when you told her you loved her?"

Silence.

"Daddy, you didn't tell her!"

"I couldn't. She wouldn't believe me."

"Yes, she would. I believed you."

"I know. It's just—"

Sabrina was near tears, but for the first time in months, they were from happiness, not pain. He loved her. *Her.* Was it true? Could she believe?

"Go," Anastasia was saying. "Go right now and tell her the truth. She has to know. You brought her a flower at the airport."

"Ah, yes, the universal love symbol."

"Daddy! I'm serious."

"Very well. I'll tell her, if only because I should have when I proposed. I was afraid to say it, but she deserves to hear it. Even if it doesn't matter to her."

Sabrina headed for the stairs. She barely made it into her room when she heard Cal climbing up behind her. She quickly brushed her cheeks and hoped that he couldn't tell she'd been crying, then reminded herself that even if he could, he would think that it was because she was sad.

There was a knock on her door. She braced herself against the window and tried to smile.

"C-come in." Her voice cracked. Had he noticed? Did it matter?

He entered the room. He was, she thought, the most perfect man ever created. So handsome and strong, so amazing.

He gave her a half smile that faded as quickly as it began. "Sabrina, I have something to tell you. I should have said it before. It's just, I was afraid." He shoved his hands into his shorts pockets. "I was just telling Anastasia that I didn't have much to recommend myself to you and I guess this proves it. I'm just some good ol' boy from Texas. My family has all the trappings of success, but they're not good people. You know that better than anyone. I'm a hard worker and I play hard. I can be stubborn. But you know that, too."

He gave a short laugh. "Here I am, trying to sell myself. Pretty sad, huh?"

She shook her head. "I think it's charming. I also think you're wonderful."

He'd been staring at the ground, but now his head snapped up. "You do?"

"Yes. I have a confession to make. I, um, had a crush on you when I first came to work for you. But I knew you weren't interested in me that way, so I made myself get over it." She took a step toward him. "At least, that was the plan. I did get over my crush, but not the way I wanted. Those shallow, silly feelings deepened, and I fell in love with you. Only I didn't recognize that fact until very recently."

His breath caught audibly. "Sabrina?"

"I love you, Cal. I think you're an amazing man. I didn't agree to marry you because I thought it would only be half a marriage, and that would have destroyed me. I need to be with someone who loves me back."

"I do," he said, hurrying toward her and grabbing her shoulders. "I love you, I think I always have. I respect you and admire you, and, dammit, I want to spend the rest of my life with you. It's not about work or Anastasia. I'll hire a new assistant and a housekeeper and a nanny if that's what it takes to convince you."

She stared at the love burning bright in his dark eyes. "I believe you. To think we spent all this time not knowing."

He kissed her hard, then drew back. "I nearly lost you. I didn't know I had you and then I could have lost you. I wouldn't have survived."

"Oh, Cal."

She wrapped her arms around his neck and pressed her lips to his. The kiss went on for a long time. When at last they surfaced, he said, "What about the job offers?"

"Is that by way of another proposal?"

"If you want it to be." He touched her cheek. "I love you, Sabrina. Would you do me the honor of becoming my wife?"

"Yes."

"You still want to work for me, too? It's only summer. We do have a half year left on our stock bet."

She laughed. "I'm going to kick your butt on that one…again."

"Cheap talk, woman."

"You lost last year, and yes, I do want to keep working for you. I might have to cut back on my hours because of your daughter, but that's okay with me, if it's okay with you."

"It's more than okay. It's wonderful."

He held her close. She sighed with contentment. Who would have thought it would come to this?

"I was thinking," she said. "How about a honeymoon in Hawaii? We could take Ada and her nieces. That way Anastasia would have someone to play with, and she would have a good time, too."

"Because it's too soon to leave her alone."

She nodded.

He tucked her hair behind her ears. "This is why I love you, Sabrina. You are the best part of me."

"And you're the best part of me." She had a thought and giggled. "*Prominence Magazine* is going to be upset. Talk about a short-lived career as an eligible bachelor. You'll be married before the issue hits the stands."

"They'll have to get over it. I'm committed to you. For life."

"For life," she echoed. "Let's go tell Anastasia. She'll be thrilled."

"Are you kidding? She already knows. She's probably arranged the entire wedding by now."

"The alternative is her going on that skating date with a boy."

"She's not dating until she's thirty. Do you hear me? Neither are all the other daughters we have together."

She laughed as they walked down the stairs. It was barely eight o'clock in the morning, and it already promised to be the most wonderful day of her life.

*   *   *   *   *

Here's a preview of next month's

Kieran O'Hara
the secret agent lover from
AGENT OF THE BLACK WATCH

by
BJ James

"Beau Anna Cahill," Tabitha scolded. "You mind your aunt Tabby and bring you sassy behind down from that rigging this minute. Time you quit playing pirate and behaved."

There was silence as Kieran O'Hara turned to stare at the ancient black woman. Not because she referred to herself as the stubborn Miss Cahill's aunt, but for the eerie sensation that she had plucked his thoughts from his mind.

He was beginning to believe this would be an interesting case. Perhaps more interesting than any before.

"What I don't understand is why I'm supposed to meet Mr. Wonderful at the dock and escort him to the cottage. Even a fool and a mainlander could find the way. Tell you what, Tabby." The strain in Beau's voice was replaced by laughter. "Just for you, I'll be so beguiling Mr. Wonderful won't know what hit him." Giving a grunt of satisfaction as the sail stayed in place, she stepped into view, keeping her back to them as she clambered down.

Moving easily in her precarious descent, she tossed comments over her shoulder. "By the way, I do need to get by the wharf. The mail boat was to bring the current copy of *Prominence Magazine*. Want to get a look at the newest heartthrob before he arrives. To immunize myself, so I don't swoon at his feet."

The last was delivered with sly sarcasm. Tabby turned toward Kieran, shrugged, then chuckled, but made no effort to stem the tide.

Stopping, she turned, scanning the dock and the steps. "What did I do with my shoes? I tied the strings together so I wouldn't keep losing one. So now I lose both."

"If you'd wear your glasses, you'd see." This time Tabby's scolding was delivered fondly, in a frequent point of contention.

"Looking for these?" Though he was enjoying the conversation and the view, spying the worn sneakers, Kieran abandoned his vantage and moved into the friendly fray.

"I beg your pardon?" Pausing in her scrambling search, Beau stared at the shoes.

"They're small, the strings are tied together," Kieran said dryly, as he glimpsed a bit of tanned forehead that was, as he'd imagined, banded by a scarf tied at a rakish angle. Though securely fixed to keep her hair from her eyes, the scarf did nothing to contain the wild, ravishing mass that flew about her shoulders, inviting a smoothing caress. Tempting Kieran.

Reining in errant thoughts, he inched the shoes closer. "They fit the description, so, I thought they were what you're looking for?"

She made no move to take them as her head tilted and eyes the color of a stormy sea lifted a dreamy, unfocused gaze to his. Blinking against the brilliance of the sun, she rose in loose-limbed and effortless ease.

Shoes and Tabby forgotten, she stood peering at him. A small woman with the hair of a fey gypsy, dressed like a tattered tomboy rather than the elegant chatelaine she'd promised. Her face was smooth, without any nuance of expression, until the faint line of a puzzled frown appeared between her brows. Dark lashes drifted down, veiling her eyes. When they lifted again, her gaze sharpened, focused. The dreamy look was replaced by uneasy concern.

For a second time she stared at him, eyes solemn and studious, then stunned by turns.

"Oops," Beau muttered, half aloud and half to herself, as she continued to stare. She didn't need an introduction to know who he was. At least, if he wasn't the man she assumed, *Prominence* had missed a sure bet. "Mr. O'Hara, I presume."

Kieran bowed in acknowledgment. "In person and at your service, Miss Cahill."

His gallantry went unnoticed.

"You weren't due until noon." Her softly accented words bore an accusation.

"I caught an earlier plane."

"But the first launch isn't until…"

"The mailman gave me a lift."

"Ohh."

"Sorry." Kieran shrugged and smiled. "It isn't noon, but I'm here."

Frown lines deepened. "Yes you are."

"I can leave and come back," he suggested, with a trace of irony. "At a more convenient time."

"There isn't one. I mean…" He'd put her at a disadvantage and she was babbling. There was nothing she hated more than babbling. Silently, she counted to ten, then back to one. Sighing, she faced what she must. "I don't suppose I should fool myself into thinking you didn't hear every word just now?"

Kieran's gaze never turned from hers. "My hearing's twenty-twenty."

The allusion to her conversation with Tabby didn't miss its mark. Hoping he would think the heat in her cheeks was from wind and sun, she suggested tentatively, "I don't suppose an apology would help."

"No."

His blunt answer took her by surprise, until she recognized the humor in his eyes. His gorgeous eyes. But then, she admitted after another slow perusal, they simply matched the rest of him. He was gorgeous all over, from the shaggy, windblown hair as black as her own, to the tips of his spanking new deck shoes.

"No apology," she agreed, determined to make the best of an awkward circumstance. "I didn't think so."

Kieran waited. The next move was hers.

"In that case, I won't try." Taking the shoes from him, she tossed them over her shoulder. Leaving one to dangle down her back and the other over her breast, she offered a hand. "Shall we start again? A truce, Mr. O'Hara?"

"Mr. O'Hara? That's twice you called me that." A brow arched, lips curled, flashing a dimple at the edge of his mouth. "I've been demoted?"

The flush deepened and there was no chance it could be mistaken for a touch of sun. Standing tall, she brazened it through. "I thought you would prefer it."

Tearing his attention from her face, Kieran studied her hand. An interesting hand, tanned, delicately formed, but he wouldn't be foolish enough to doubt its strength. "I prefer Kieran, the name my friends call me."

His speculative gaze trailed over her in a lingering study before lifting again to hers. Holding her with a magnetism that was inescapable, he spoke in a voice as soothing as a whisper. "We're going to be friends, you know."

Hearing a serious note beneath the teasing, Beau said nothing as the tide lapped at the shore, the wind danced among sails, and Tabby stood listening.

Kieran moved closer, concentrating intently on her mouth, ignoring her proffered hand. "Friends, Beau Anna?"

Jerking back as her fingers touched his belt, she was acutely conscious of every nuance in his look and his voice. A part of her was drawn to him, a part wanted to retreat. Gathering her wits, she held her ground.

He was a charming one, with an irresistible grin and an elegant old-world gallantry. Beau didn't question that he knew exactly how charming. How elegant. How gallant. But he was only here for the summer, and she could deal with that, too.

"All right." With an attitude meant to be nonchalant, she accepted the challenge. "I won't make promises, but we can try."

"I can't ask for more than that." Catching her hand, he enveloped it in his. His grip was considerate, but his palm was hard and ridged against hers as he kept it with a subtle pressure. "No promises. For now."

SILHOUETTE®

Desire®

Do you want...

Dangerously handsome heroes

Evocative, everlasting love stories

Sizzling and tantalizing sensuality

Incredibly sexy miniseries like **MAN OF THE MONTH**

Red-hot romance

Enticing entertainment that can't be beat!

You'll find all of this, and much *more* each and every month in **SILHOUETTE DESIRE**. Don't miss these unforgettable love stories by some of romance's hottest authors. Silhouette Desire—where your fantasies will always come true....

INTIMATE MOMENTS ®

Silhouette ®

If you've got the time...
We've got the
INTIMATE MOMENTS

Passion. Suspense. Desire. Drama. Enter a world that's larger than life, where men and women overcome life's greatest odds for the ultimate prize: love. Nonstop excitement is closer than you think...in Silhouette Intimate Moments!

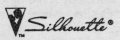
Silhouette ®

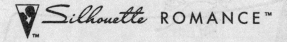

What's a single dad to do when he needs a wife by next Thursday?

Who's a confirmed bachelor to call when he finds a baby on his doorstep?

How does a plain Jane in love with her gorgeous boss get him to notice her?

From classic love stories to romantic comedies to emotional heart tuggers, **Silhouette Romance** offers six irresistible novels every month by some of your favorite authors! Such as...beloved bestsellers **Diana Palmer, Annette Broadrick, Suzanne Carey, Elizabeth August** and **Marie Ferrarella**, to name just a few—and some sure to become favorites!

Fabulous Fathers...Bundles of Joy...Miniseries... Months of blushing brides and convenient weddings... Holiday celebrations... You'll find all this and much more in **Silhouette Romance**—always emotional, always enjoyable, always about love!

WAYS TO *UNEXPECTEDLY* MEET MR. RIGHT:

♡ Go out with the sexy-sounding stranger your daughter secretly set you up with through a personal ad.

♡ RSVP yes to a wedding invitation—soon it might be your turn to say "I do!"

♡ Receive a marriage proposal by mail— from a man you've never met....

These are just a few of the unexpected ways that written communication leads to love in Silhouette Yours Truly.

Each month, look for two fast-paced, fun and flirtatious Yours Truly novels (with entertaining treats and sneak previews in the back pages) by some of your favorite authors—and some who are sure to become favorites.

YOURS TRULY™:
Love—when you least expect it!